# Call Center Freak

# Call Center Freak

*Kaylha Karrington*

www.urbanbooks.net

Urban Books, LLC
300 Farmingdale Road, N.Y.-Route 109
Farmingdale, NY 11735

ISBN 13: 978-1-64556-596-3
EBOOK ISBN: 978-1-64556-597-0

First Trade Paperback Printing May 2024
Printed in the United States of America

10 9 8 7 6 5 4 3 2 1

Distributed by Kensington Publishing Corp.
Submit Orders to:
Customer Service
400 Hahn Road
Westminster, MD 21157-4627
Phone: 1-800-733-3000
Fax: 1-800-659-2436

# Call Center Freak

by

*Kaylha Karrington*

# Prologue

The burning smell of the smoking gun flowed up into his nostrils along with the warm night air. He thought it was appropriate. A mirror to the rage that had consumed his mind for the last few hours—his marriage had deteriorated into a cold and godless union. Lying prostrate before him was the writhing body of the man who had stolen his life from him and robbed him of everything that he'd worked so hard for. He stood there emotionless, watching the thief of his livelihood tremble while begging for mercy not to shoot again. His words sounded like the low moans of a wounded animal.

"What the fuck are you doing, man? Please don't kill me. *Please!*" The man pleaded for his life as he struggled to breathe.

The gray concrete walls of the low-lit parking garage seemed to be closing in on the victim. He tried to reach out to his attacker for mercy, but he was forced to put pressure on his wound, which was gushing blood onto the cold ground beneath him. He had always known that his lifestyle would catch up to him someday—but he never imagined it would be like this. He could feel the heat from the bullet searing through his stomach and searching to make its way out of his back. He wondered if the man now standing over him just wanted him to suffer or if he was really just that bad of a shot. The pain was like nothing he'd ever felt before, and it intensified as time seemed to begin to slow down with every second that passed.

The gunman began to panic and sweat with confusion from possible regret. He started pacing back and forth, revisiting the idea that he'd come here to end this man's life for what he had done. But if he didn't finish him off, it would all be for nothing, and in his head, the victim just might win again. Could he do it? Would he finish the job that he set out to do? Nervously shaking while raising the gun, he took one last look at his victim, closed his eyes, took a deep breath, and mustered the courage to pull the trigger for the second . . . and final time.

# Chapter 1

*Three Years Earlier* . . .

"Nigga, I can't believe I'm about to do this shit," Damond spoke. He had been drinking all day and was feeling rather sentimental. "Shit, I can't believe *she* about to do this shit. I mean, can you imagine any woman marrying a bum-ass nigga like me? Like she's really gonna love me forever-ever, forever-ever?"

Sean couldn't help but cackle while he hoisted up his boy onto the balcony of the penthouse suite at the Westin Hotel. He and Damond had been partners for as long as he could remember. They did practically everything together and had chased girls, only to love 'em and leave 'em alone. And now, his partner in crime was ready to throw in the towel and finally settle down.

"Yeah, nigga, she gonna marry you all right . . . and have a shit ton of big, bobble-headed-ass babies running around here look'n just like yo' high yella ass." Sean shifted himself so he could try to sit Damond's heavy-weight ass in one of the patio chairs, hoping he could sober him up before the main festivities began. Sean wanted him coherent enough to be at least able to enjoy himself, even if he was too fucked up to remember any of it. Damond just kept on ranting—unaware that he was even sitting. Sean quickly ran inside, searching for a bottle of water to give Damond, something to get him sobered up quickly.

"Yeah, man, Tia really love my ass. And, nigga, she's a good woman too. Like, bruh, she is actually smart as fuck, *and*-and she fine as hell. I guess you could say a nigga like me is winning. And, bruh, dem pretty-ass titties just be sittin' at attention anytime she sees a nigga too. She be thinking that a nigga don't notice 'em. And dat *ass,* my nigga. Bruh, dat ass is so phat, nigga. I swear to God, my dick be instantly getting hard on sight, ya heard me? I just love watching her ass ripple up like the ocean when I be smashing dat shit." Damond tried to stand as he imitated a thrusting motion. Instead, he staggered, then settled back into the patio chair, beaming, when a sickening thought struck him. "Ay, man, but I'm tellin' you now, though, she betta be hittin' da gym wit' er'ry one of dem big-headed-ass kids! Shiiiiit, I don't care what she gotta do—because I ain't fuckin' no big, nasty, Rasputia-lookin'-ass bitch . . . Ewwww, man. I'ma throw up just thinkin' about that shit." He made a gagging sound when another thought crossed his mind. "But, my nigga, did I tell you ever since I taught that ho how to breathe out of her nose . . . while she giving me head . . . she been deep-throating a nigga on some supahead-type shit, man? Damn, that shit be good as fuck."

"Who, nigga? Tia or Rasputia?" Sean asked as he returned soon enough to catch the last of Damond's rant. He chuckled and opened the Fiji water bottle, handing it to Damond. "Here, man, just shut the fuck up and drink the damn water. You so fucked up, bruh, you 'bout to fuck around and miss the grand finale of your own party."

"I'm saying, Sean, Sean! Supahead status, my nigga." Damond cackled, spilling half the bottle of water on the patio. "Damn, my baby *loves* me. Oooh weee, I'm 'bout to marry me a supahead." Damond snickered just thinking about Tia's head game.

"Drink the damn water, man." Sean had seen his boy fucked up before. College had seen the best and worst of them both . . . but this shit was ridiculous. He could only imagine what the idea of getting married was doing to his boy, and the alcohol was the only escape from the reality of it all for now. That and the nice surprise Sean had lined up—just to take everybody's mind off the purpose of the gathering. Damond would be married by Sunday, but today was Friday, and there was nothing like that last "taste" before the Big Day.

Suddenly, someone knocked on the hotel door.

"Hey, was that the door? Somebody cut down the damn music," Sean yelled, but nobody moved.

*Knock, knock, knock.*

Sean glanced back at Damond, still sitting, gazing out at the night lights, calmly drinking his water in sort of a daze.

"Hey, my nigga, come in here—off the patio. You done got enough fresh air, and besides, I got something for ya."

Damond didn't protest. He just stood up and wrapped his arm around Sean's neck again. "My nigga. You know you my nigga, right?" he said, pounding Sean's chest with the open water bottle, spilling what was left.

"Ayo, cut the muh'fuckin' music down when my nigga say cut the muh'fuckin' music down. My nigga say he got a surprise for me, and I'm tryin'a see, gotdammit!" Damond yelled, slurring every other word.

The music was quickly paused.

The knocking continued on the hotel room door.

"Hey, Sway, open the damn door, nigga . . . Let's see what *'room service'* got for the man of the hour." Sean dragged one of the Victorian-style office chairs in the middle of the room and sat Damond down in it. The men in the room started going crazy, knowing how Damond's crew rolled . . . It was, after all, a bachelor's party.

Sway opened the door, and it was like the floodgates of heaven just opened.

Every woman that poured into the room looked like they belonged on the cover of an XXX magazine—the baddest of bitches that Instagram would have to offer. Five, then eight, and then twelve, nearly twenty girls filled the room. The group of guys began to make way, parting like the Red Sea as the twenty sexy-ass females made a circle around Damond's throne. The women lined themselves up by him and posed as if they were auditioning for a Miss America pageant rather than the real debauchery they were about to get into. But Sean knew what type of women his boy liked, and this was a virtual smorgasbord of pros. Only the finest and the best of the best that the QC had to offer.

Sean shook his head and grabbed the props he had stashed in the room. He placed the costume crown on Damond's head and began to announce, "My niggas, let me welcome you all to the Frasier-Freak-Nasty Contest." The room began to roar at the announcement. Sean let the energy build while the men howled and gawked at the caliber and abundance of ass that had just entered the room. He too was even impressed, shaking his head at just how gorgeous every single lady there was. The newly crowned Damond rubbed his hands together like a man who'd just won the megamillion lottery . . . or like Birdman.

"Ay, somebody pass me a bottle, man. I'm starting to get too sober around this bitch," Damond yelled. He could feel the liquor beginning to wear off a bit and wanted to get his buzz back.

Sean walked over to the stereo station and scrolled through the playlist he created for the night, trying to find the perfect song. He wanted to play something that he knew would get the women hyped so they would be in the mood to dance and shake their asses off. He scrolled quickly and then came across a classic . . . Pastor Troy's "Pop that Pussy" began to rumble through the speakers. The women looked at each other and smiled, tickled by the song choice but excited to each take turns with Damond, working their bodies and pulsating to the music, vying for his attention. Damond's friends stood on the chairs and sofas, trying to glimpse the ladies' performances, wishing they were the ones sitting on the throne. The guys howled and pounded each other as they deliberated about which one was the baddest bitch. Damond stood and motioned for a few other ladies to begin their bodies poppin'.

"Now, D . . . There are some hungry-ass wolves all around you . . . They salivating, bruh." The men erupted in barks and howls. "And they are *hungry* for some of these sweet tenders you got standing here. So, since you are the man of the hour, take your pick, my nigga, or *I* will," Sean said while rubbing his hands together, already imagining his top pick and just what he would do to her. "But, my nigga, real talk, you are 'The Muhfuckin' Man of the Hour' that will single-handedly choose the winner of this here Frasier-Freak-Nasty Contest," Sean teased. "The talent portion will commence directly after—but I don't even know how you gon' pick, Black man, 'cause deez hoes is *fine* and *talented*."

The crowd roared as Damond began to scan the thighs, asses, and faces of the women surrounding him. The women coiled and writhed their bodies, licking their lips and flicking their tongues.

"Damn." Damond couldn't pick . . . Each one was sexier than the next, and all of them trumped Tia in the Bad Bitch Department.

"Tell you what, ladies. Turn around . . . gon' head and let daddy see them asses and how they bounce," Sean instructed.

One by one, each dancer slowly began to turn while removing their tops and making their asses ripple like the waves in the ocean. Again, the room went crazy with roars from the fellas until Sean noticed one that kept her top on. She had a baby face, but Sean knew his hookup was reputable, so she had to be at least 18. Besides, the boys weren't into hella young girls anyway. Wasn't nobody trying to catch a case.

Damond's eyes fell on the same thick, doe-eyed girl with long, curly, jet-black hair and the body of a goddess. Her skin was the color of caramel, so creamy and soft looking. Not a blemish in sight, and the tiny, green, two-piece that gripped her curves barely covered the tiny hummingbird tattoo on her hip.

"What's wrong, mama? You don't wanna play?" Damond reached to grab her hand, spinning her around to get a closer look. "What's your name, love, and how old are you with this baby face?" Damond lifted his hand, moving a strand of hair from her face.

Looking uninterested in playing the "getting to know you" game and more focused on her purpose for being there, which was her money, Niko introduced herself to Damond. "Hey, I'm Treasure, and I'm old enough, which is all you need to concern yourself with."

"Damn, ma, you feisty. Well, 'Ms. Treasure I'm Old Enough,' are you the lucky one trying to win this contest?" Damond sipped his water, continuing to slowly scan her body. "You know you wanna win, pretty lady."

"Oh, I'll win," Niko confidently answered as she leaned toward Damond, slowly and sensually. She moved with the sleekness of a panther hunting her prey. Niko pushed Damond back into the chair, straddling his thighs and leaning in to whisper in his ear. "'Cause once you taste this pussy, daddy . . . You'll know why they call me 'Treasure,' and that's a promise," she said while placing soft kisses on Damond's neck and gently licking the edge of his ear. She then pulled back just enough to slide her long tongue over his soft, sexy lips, dipping her tongue inside of his mouth, caressing his tongue with hers.

Everyone was in awe at the slight performance happening right before their eyes. Sean couldn't believe the baddest chick in the group had picked Damond.

Niko knew she was turning Damond on because she could feel his dick growing inside of his pants while she was on top of him. She stood up, turning around to give Damond a closer look at her tiny waist and plump ass that complemented her soft, thick thighs. Niko slid her ass against Damond's chest, slowly gyrating down onto his lap. He could feel the heat from her pussy radiating from between her thighs. Niko stood up, blew a kiss, and winked before she walked away. Damond looked like a deer in headlights. Niko's sexual advances so turned him on that he sat there with his mouth wide open yet speechless.

Niko turned around, looking into Damond's eyes. "What's wrong, papi? You having second thoughts about exploring Treasure?" Damond swallowed. Her confidence and tone had him at a loss for words, but there was no way he was going to be punked by a stripper.

Damond stood up, reaching his hand toward Niko to come with him. She smiled because she knew that there was no way that Damond would let her get away now. Niko pushed him back into the seat, this time straddling Damond by wrapping her legs around his waist. Like a kitten, she purred, placing small kisses on Damond's neck, again leading up to his ear, sucking and licking on his earlobe. He pushed himself up, holding on to Niko by grabbing her by her soft, round ass, and carried her into the next room.

Sean attempted to stop Damond. "My nigga, you know you ain't gotta pick her or even just one. I got you like mad bad bitches to choose from in this muhfucka," Sean yelled and then gave their friend Sway dap. He took a sip of his beer. *He* wanted to be the one taking a trip to Treasure Island. *She is fine as hell,* Sean thought to himself, but for this time only, he was willing to pass up Treasure so that his boy could enjoy another bitch's pussy one last time before saying, "I do."

Once in the room, before Damond could make the first move, Niko kicked off her shoes and took Damond's hand, sliding it down into the front of her bikini bottom so that he could feel her warm juices flooding her pussy. Damond was again left speechless but maintained his composure because he didn't want Niko to feel like she was in control. Niko pushed him onto the bed and began climbing on top of him. She slowly slid her body up across his abdomen until she was positioned sitting on his chest. She locked her thick thighs in place over his arms, leaning in and taking his bottom lip in her mouth, teasing his mouth with her tongue. Niko then stood up on the bed directly over Damond's face, placing one foot on each side of his head.

Looking up at Niko, Damond could see the thin green material of her bikini bottom was soaked, with her phat pussy lips hanging out of each side of the crotch. Damond could hear the "damns" coming from his friends in the other room. If he was tipsy before, she had just completely sobered him up. She began making her ass clap, dropping it low over Damond's face, teasing him with the sweet scent of her pussy and the jiggle of her bouncing ass in his face.

Looking down at Damond, she smiled and asked, "Do I win now, papi?" seeking confirmation, as her primary focus was on the cash winnings more than anything else.

Damond didn't respond because all he could focus on was the wet pussy standing over him and fucking the shit out of Treasure.

The fellas in the other room erupted with hands clapping and catcalling as everyone witnessed what had just gone down because the room door had been left open.

Damond didn't realize how much he was sweating until Niko removed her bikini top. He began to dab the sweat beads from his forehead. Sean and the others stared in admiration because they could tell Damond was in for a wild treat.

"Damn, nigga, you scared?" Sean yelled from the next room. "You looking like you might need some help with this one," he said jokingly, although deep down, he would have loved to get a piece of Treasure by himself.

Damond licked his lips and shook his head. He looked at Treasure, nodding toward the door, gesturing for her to close it. Everyone and everything disappeared from Damond's thoughts as the door shut, including the fact that he would become Tia's husband the following day.

Sean had never witnessed his boy respond to a female in that way. He went and knocked on the door. "Yo, bruh, when you hittin' that shit, tell that trick to look back at it," he laughed and stared at the door, wishing it were him on the other side and not Damond.

Damond had to steady himself. He was staring into Niko's beautiful brown eyes. She noticed his hard dick through his pants while he was lying back, waiting for her to return to him. She climbed back on top of Damond, this time perfectly positioning her pussy directly on top of his rock-hard dick. She began to grind on him, moaning while playing with her hard nipples. The smell of her hair was even turning him on. It smelled of sweet coconut and mango. Damond couldn't help but think how the smell complemented her exotic look. He sat up face-to-face with her, looking into her eyes as if he could see straight through to her soul. She moaned as his hand traveled between her legs, seeking out her growing clitoris. His head was slightly spinning from all of the alcohol he had previously consumed. However, all he could focus on was the aroma of her natural pheromones and how he was about to give her the business.

She pushed her breast in his face, using her nipple to caress his soft lips gently. Damond could feel himself becoming more excited. Niko pushed him back on the bed, again keeping her hips locked in position. He closed his eyes, sighing with satisfaction, enjoying the vibrations of her movements against him. Then, suddenly, he felt her weight shift, and the warmth of her body disappeared from him. He opened his eyes to see her standing at the foot of the bed.

"Hey, hey, whatcha doing, boo?" he questioned.

Niko grinned, selfishly opening the palm of her hand. One thing was for sure. Niko was always about her money, no matter what, and nothing, not even good sex, would get in the way of it.

"I won, daddy, so I need to get my prize before I let you get into the Treasure."

"Nah, nah, I'm the man of the hour. Don't ruin the moment talking about no little bit of money."

"Your boy said the winner gets paid, and I ain't doing nothing if I ain't gettin' paid." Niko began walking toward the door. Damond felt his stomach tighten as panic set in as he watched her walk away. He grabbed his cell to text Sean. Man, come in here. She trippin'.

As Niko touched the knob to turn it, the door opened. Sean was standing there with a smile on his face. Niko was not up for any shenanigans. She came for one thing and one thing only. "You and your boy need to get it together. I ain't doin' shit without my money. I ain't here for these games. I need my funds, or I ain't doin' nothing. I'm 'bout to be out," Niko said, giving Sean the side-eye before attempting to exit the room.

Sean grabbed Niko's arm. She glared at him with a scathing look, and he quickly let go. "Hey, hey, what's going on, baby doll? Calm down, shorty. We got you. Why you trippin'?" Sean asked.

Niko took a deep breath and turned to Sean. "Look here, I made a deal, and it seems like y'all lame-ass niggas can't hold your end of the bargain," she scoffed. "I should have known y'all niggas was on some broke-boy shit. All I know is ain't nothin' goin' down without me being cashed out. A deal is a deal, and Treasure don't be fucking for free. I'm the winner, so I'ma need the winner's prize money up front. I know how y'all niggas like to do, and I can tell you now, this one ain't the bitch y'all niggas gon' get over on today." It was evident that Niko was becoming equally frustrated and ready to leave.

"Now, look here, shawty. It ain't even like that. I already paid Moose," Sean said, trying to get Niko to calm down and get back to business.

Without skipping a beat, Niko rolled her eyes at Sean. "Ooh . . . Okay. Well, you need to call Moose and have Moose come fuck him then. I was told it was a bonus for the bitch that was selected to *treat* the groom-to-be, so I either get my rack now, or I bounce, simple as that . . . or you can get one of these lame hoes to come play for free," Niko said, pointing to the room where the other girls were entertaining. "My pussy don't get wet for no free shit. Matter a fact, how about I just call Moose myself and tell him what y'all niggas in here trying to do?"

"No, now, wait, wait. I got your money, baby girl," Sean said with concern.

Neither Sean nor Damond wanted problems with Moose. He was known as the city's "Frank Lucas." Moose was *that* dude, and everyone knew it. He had a heart of gold, but one thing you didn't mess with was his money and his connects. Moose looked after Niko as if she were his little sister, and he would never allow anyone to hurt her or take advantage of her.

Reaching down into his pockets, Sean looked over at Damond. "Damn, this party is really digging into a nigga pockets, bruh."

Niko had mastered the art of private parties. She wasn't new to the game Sean and Damond were trying to play.

Sean then thought to himself that he was going to make sure that *he* and his boy were going to get their stack worth out of Niko's pretty little ass. He handed her the money . . . She snatched it from him and began counting it. "Damn, you gonna do that right in my face like I'm some sort of lame-ass nigga?"

"Yup. It's a must that I make sure all my cash is here before services are rendered." She continued counting as she opened the door, gesturing for Sean to leave. "A'ight, we straight now, so you can leave."

"Oh no, boo. I'm staying to at least watch this performance, and it better be worth that damn rack too," Sean said while taking a sip of his beer.

"Ooh nah, this ain't no show, boo. You gots to go or pay extra just to watch this Treasure."

Sean moved toward her. Niko held her phone up, hitting the speaker icon, then facing it toward Sean, showing him that her phone was making a connecting call to Moose.

"What up, Treasure? Something wrong?" the deep male voice answered.

"Hey, Buddha, I got this lame over here trying to do some slick shit," she said while glaring at Sean.

"A'ight. You still at that spot? I'ma come through, get it all straightened out."

Sean interrupted, yelling toward the phone, "Nah, no. Wait, Moose. I got you, big man. I just wanted to make sure my boy was straight." Sean looked over at Damond, who nodded to him, confirming that he was straight. The uncalled-for exchange had killed the little buzz that Damond had left. Sean walked slowly toward the door. He paused, only to smack Treasure on her ass. She slammed the door in his face and placed the money in her wristlet pouch.

"OK, Buddha, we good over here," she said, putting the phone to her ear.

"All right, baby girl. Hit me if you need me."

Niko hung up the phone and turned to face Damond. She smirked. "Now that we got that shit out da way . . ." She slid the lime-green bikini bottom off. "And just so you know, nigga, we ain't about to be making love up in this bitch. We straight fuckin', so you might as well put something on that I can bounce this ass to. Shit, I know that's what you wanna see anyway."

Damond licked his lips as he watched her ass jiggle while she walked across the room. He was so mesmerized by her flawless body that he fumbled with the stereo's remote. She took the remote from him and searched through the track list until she found the perfect track for the occasion. Plies song, "Fucking Or What," began to blare from the stereo. "What you know 'bout this, daddy?" Niko asked.

"Come here, and I'ma show you," Damond said as he removed his shirt and motioned for her to come to him.

Niko smiled seductively and licked her lips. He was fine as hell, and that she couldn't deny. She didn't take up many of these bonus offers, but she was relieved to have a client that she could actually enjoy for once. Sex was like a conquest for her because she knew her skills were impeccable. She felt empowered being able to make a man scream and watch his toes curl. So, if she could make some fast cash occasionally for doing something she loved, she was definitely up for it.

Niko knew that she was going to enjoy this encounter with Damond. He had a large tattoo that covered his sculpted chest and part of his chiseled abdomen. She pushed him back onto the bed and began to straddle his lap. She began to take a closer look at his tattoo and noticed that it was similar to a sphinx, half of Damond's face and half of a lion's face. She had never seen anything like it, and for some reason, it caused a chill to run up her spine. Damond reached down, gripping her hips and pulling her forward until her pussy slid down his chest, then over his face. He inhaled the floral scent radiating from her warm, sweet pussy and licked his lips.

"Damn, what kind of sweetness you got up in there? That shit smell good as fuck, shorty. I got to taste that baby." Damond was eager to get his tongue inside of Niko.

Niko smirked at the corny line, but Damond's sexiness so turned her on she couldn't wait to feel his tongue up against her throbbing clit.

He grabbed her ass and plunged his long, thick tongue deep inside her.

She gasped as it penetrated her. "Ooooh, fuuuuck!"

His stiff tongue moved in and out with long, slow strokes. He formed a hook with his tongue so that each time he slid it out, it would graze her clitoris. His tongue was so thick and long that she found herself pumping her pussy on it as if she were riding a dick. *Damn, what kind of freak is this nigga?* she thought. The heat from his warm tongue and the passionate flicks of his tongue made her cry out with her first orgasm. She tried to pull away as her creaminess flooded his mouth, but she couldn't get away.

Damond grabbed Niko's waist, briskly flipping her over on the bed, and began pulling her firm body closer to his. He sat up just enough to admire her beautiful body again. Damond still couldn't believe just how perfect Niko's body was. He began to lick her perky nipples that were standing at attention from uninterrupted arousal. The riffle of his tongue was driving her crazy. Niko couldn't help but think just how good his dick was going to be.

Damond was so caught up in his actions that he flipped Niko over onto her stomach. He brought her to her knees, keeping her head firmly placed on the pillow. Niko couldn't help but arch her back while her ass opened up, revealing just what Damond was looking for. Keeping her legs open, his tongue began cuffing her clitoris from behind. She clawed at the bed, trying to regain control and escape his tongue. He laughed at her, forcefully jerking her back into position.

"Damn, that is some sweet pussy," he said while sliding his middle finger into her dripping pussy, checking to see if she was ready for war. "Don't fucking run from me, girl. I want you to come for me again. Drip it on my tongue, babe."

He opened her lips wider, taking her fully exposed clit into his mouth, sucking and licking harder and faster while massaging the inside of her vaginal walls with his long, thick fingers. Her pussy was so wet that Damond's hand was covered in ecstasy.

Niko couldn't hold out any longer, yelling out, "Yeeeesss, daddy, suck this pussy." She had never had a man eat her pussy like that before. A woman could easily make her come, but never a man. She couldn't believe that real tears were coming from her eyes. She wanted to get away from his damn tongue, but her pussy was about to explode with pleasure. "Damn, nigga, fuck. Ah, I'm coming again, daddy." She bucked against his mouth and joined the rhythm of his tongue. Her sexy body shuddered for a second time.

Damond loved the way she tasted and could lick her sweet cunt all day and all night, but he couldn't wait to fulfill her request to be fucked. The sounds that escaped her lips were a real turn-on, and his dick was eager to slip deep inside of her. Damn, her pussy was addictive. He reluctantly released her, and Niko sat up, turning toward Damond. He took his cum-covered hand, placing each finger slowly in her mouth. Treasure, licking her wetness from his hand, couldn't help but agree that she tasted sweet. He loved the way she looked at him while cleaning her juices from his hand, but the look abruptly changed from a look of delight to a naughty, devilish grin.

"Okay, round one was yours, nigga. My turn . . . Stand right here." Niko motioned for Damond to move in front of her because, now, it was her turn to take control. She loved to dominate any sexual situation, and she knew she was very good at it.

Niko handed him a small gold packet she had taken from her wristlet. She slithered down to the foot of the bed . . . unbuckled his belt, and unzipped his pants. His pants fell to the floor, and he eagerly stepped out of them. She smiled and slightly bit her lip as his long pipe bounced out of the top of his briefs. She stood up and grabbed his hand, walking him over to the full-length mirror in the room.

She looked into his eyes and said, "We need the mirror because I love to watch myself perform."

Niko slid down to her knees, gently reached up, and grabbed his rock-hard dick. She ran her tongue gently up his dick, slowly making her way to the head. She was initially daunted by the size of his cock because of its thickness and width. However, she couldn't let him know of her distress, so she wrapped her pretty lips around the head of his dick, slowly taking him in her warm, wet mouth. His dick was so sensitive that he shifted his legs just to keep his balance.

Damond's head fell backward as he began to moan while her mouth pleased him, moving up and down the shaft of his fully extended dick. Niko had the perfect rhythm, warmth, and wetness to offer Damond's dick. It was so perfect that Damond felt his legs getting weaker and weaker with each stroke of her mouth. He couldn't help but glance at her in the mirror. He knew he needed to sit down as she was making him weak, and watching her take all of him in her mouth wasn't helping. Niko was going to make him come quickly, he thought.

In an attempt to throw his focus, Damond looked down at Niko. "Hey, babe, I'm still a little fucked up. How 'bout we take this back to the bed?" he asked, trying to conceal the fact that Niko's head game was on point. Although he initially considered his fiancée to be a super-head, after tonight's performance, Niko just bumped Tia to second place.

Niko smiled because she felt his legs trembling the entire time. She agreed to move to the bed, but not before giving him three more long, deep strokes of the throat just to let him know what she had in store for him.

They moved back to the bed, and he felt something warm and wet on his balls. "Aaah, damn." Damond couldn't hold back.

It was her soft tongue caressing the area between his sack and his ass. The position was a bit awkward for him, but it felt so good that he didn't want her to stop. Niko was sucking and licking in spots where his soon-to-be wife never ventured. She moved her mouth to his sack, creating a vibrating sensation, and could feel his nuts twitching in her mouth from the stimulation.

"Don't come yet, daddy," Niko whispered, looking up at him with her beautiful brown eyes. "I'm loving this big dick you 'bout to give me," she whispered, taking his manhood in her hand, still gently stroking while slowly coming to her feet in front of him. "Here, take your belt," she said, picking the belt up from the floor.

Damond was anxious as hell. He couldn't take his eyes off Niko. He was amazed at her skill level and how she managed to stimulate all the important parts of his body, something his fiancée could never do.

"Ummm, and the condom I gave you, yeah, I require it," she said, wanting him to have it on before her feet and hands were tied. Damond stared at her momentarily, still mesmerized by what was happening. Niko snapped her fingers, trying to get his focus back. "Uh, condom . . . It needs to be on."

"Oh shit, yeah, the condom." Damon grinned as he opened the gold pack, slipping on the snug condom.

She sat back on the bed, pulling her feet and hands together. "OK, now, tie the belt around my ankles and hands. I want you to beat this pussy up for me, babe. Can you do that, daddy? Give me all that dick for your last night of freedom, baby," Niko requested while holding her wrists near her ankles, waiting for Damond to do as he was told.

With excitement in his eyes, Damond took the belt from Niko's hands and began tying her ankles and wrists together. Niko then lay back on the bed, pulling her tied ankles and wrists all the way back behind her head, locking them with ease, exposing her clean-shaven, phat pussy. Damond immediately thought to himself, *This bitch is limber as fuck, and I'm 'bout to tear this pussy up.*

He leaned in to mount Niko and nearly lost his balance as he slid his dick into her soaked box. He couldn't help but think, *For a stripper, her pussy is so tight compared to the countless other strippers I've been with.* It gripped his dick like a glove each time he slid in and out, never losing its grip or loosening up like plenty of other women that he fucked. He grabbed her legs, which were still behind her head. Damond was slamming his dick into her wet love-box while gripping her legs tighter and tighter as he thrust to the beat of the song that was now playing.

"Yeah, daddy, yeah. You like watching yourself dig in this pussy?" Niko asked. "You like how this tight pussy swallows your big cock, huh?"

She had a foul mouth, but that shit turned him on even more.

Damond quickly glanced down at her pretty pink pussy, and how her juices had his dick glistening. He could feel himself becoming weaker and weaker with each stroke and words that Niko spoke.

"Do that shit, babe. Fill me up, daddy! Fuck this wet pussy, baby." Niko continued to talk nasty to him because she knew it was driving him crazy.

Damond could feel the pressure building inside of him. He was losing control as he continued to dip his dick farther inside her center.

"I love this big dick in me, daddy! Slide your finger into my ass while you stroke me, papi. I want to experience super ecstasy and come with you, daddy," Niko continued to instruct.

Damond stuck his middle finger in her ass, sending himself and Niko over the edge. He let out an almost Tarzan yell, struggling to remain in control as he filled the condom with his milk. Her pussy gripped his dick before spraying him with cum. His legs were so weak he could feel himself about to fall over. He rolled over, closing his eyes, trying to regain focus, gasping for breath.

In the other room, they could hear laughs and clapping. He opened his eyes to see the door cracked with Sean, Sway, and some other guys standing in the door. Niko was still laid back on the bed, signaling Damond to untie her. He removed the belt, and Niko glared at Sean, rolling her eyes.

Damond was still trying to catch his breath but finally stood up. He began walking toward the door, waving his hands as if to tell the fellas to leave the room.

Sean stood looking at Niko, hoping she would consider doing him next. "Nigga, is you all right? We heard you yell and just came to see if you were okay." Reaching his fist out to Damond to give him a fist bump, he said, "My gotdamn *dog* was in here tearing the pussy out of the frame! That shit looked . . . oweeee!" Sean teased Damond before being pushed out of the doorway.

Damond pushed all the men out and locked the door. Niko had excused herself into the bathroom. Damond wasn't sure if she was embarrassed by his friends catching a glimpse of their sexcapades, so he knocked on the door to check on her.

"Hey, you all right?" he asked.

"I'm straight," she replied.

He stood outside the door for a moment before putting on his underwear, then sitting at the foot of the bed. Damond was thoroughly satisfied and enjoyed every bit of his experience with Treasure.

After about fifteen minutes, Niko came out of the bathroom dressed in her bikini and a cover-up. She was attempting to fix her hair and reapply her makeup.

"Oh shit, I'm sorry. I didn't mean to fuck up your hair and makeup. You're still beautiful as fuck, though," Damond said, biting his lip, smiling at the idea of wanting more and trying to figure out just how he could get it.

"It's cool. Remember, I just earned a rack." She winked, popping a piece of gum in her mouth. Niko grabbed the last bit of her things. She picked up her phone, leaned over, and kissed Damond's forehead. "Good luck with your nuptials."

He grabbed her arm. "Wait . . . Where you going?"

Pulling away from him, making her way to the door, she said, "Um, you only get an hour, boo. I gots to go."

"Damn, you gotta be on the clock to talk to me?" Damond quickly replied.

Niko looked back at him. For a moment, she felt the urge to stay because the dick was actually good, and his head game was serious. Finally, however, she shook her head. "Sorry, this is business, and that is the first rule. I'm out."

Damond scurried for his pants, trying to hurry up and put them on before Niko left the room. He knew he didn't have any cash on him, and he also knew Sean was not about to pay her anything extra after shelling out that rack. Well, at least not without him being a part of it, and, of course, Damond did not want to share this one, that was for sure.

"Aye, though, look, baby girl . . . So how do I get in contact with you?" Damond was so serious about his inquisition.

"You don't," Niko answered. "It wouldn't be wise. Besides, you 'bout to walk down the aisle, and honestly, that is the only person you need to contact. Look, this was business for me . . . I've done this shit before, and mixing business with pleasure never works. And I definitely ain't got time for your wife and her ugly-ass homegirls coming for me, trying to check me about you. I work at the club. You can come there if you want to see me, but you ain't getting my info. Now, with that being said, I had a real nice time, and your wife is one lucky lady. Maybe you can get one of the other tricks to set you off if you got the energy, but me . . . I'm done, boo." She walked toward the door and stopped to turn and look back at Damond. "Oh, and don't forget . . . The name is Treasure."

He stood there staring at her, trying to fix his shirt, "Aye, but look, though . . . I definitely enjoyed exploring your *treasure*." The door closed, and Damond sat back on the bed as a wave of panic came over him as he thought about Sunday.

# Chapter 2

*Three Years Later . . .*

Niko danced with her reflection in the mirror. The morning mix on the radio was blaring Beyoncé's newest single. "You won't break my soul. You won't break my soul, nah nah," Niko sang as she removed her oversized white tee and stepped into the steaming shower. It was a Monday morning, and though typically, Niko wasn't a morning person, today was different. She was feeling great. New day . . . new job . . . new start, and she could hardly wait. Her new job would be the jump start she desperately needed—financially and professionally. Niko was always determined to pay her own way in life, especially now that she could finally dress the part of a "corporate professional." Things had gotten tough for her this year, battling a recession with no job, but Niko was the ideal survivor. She was focused on her grind, whether dancing, stripping, or making trips for dope boys to ATL or VA. She even provided a laundry service out of her apartment to keep from being evicted. Niko prided herself in never asking for handouts or being a needy chick.

The daughter of a Cuban father and an African American mother, she used what she had to get what she wanted. Blessed with good looks, charm, and quick wit, she could talk anyone into giving her almost anything.

And now, her undeniable intelligence seemed to be paying off finally.

Niko stepped out from the steamy shower and patted her honey-bronze skin with the towel. She wiped the steam from the mirror with her hand, removing the bobby pin from the bun at the nape of her neck. Her long, damp, curly, jet-black hair fell to her bare shoulders. Niko observed and admired her reflection in the mirror. Her nicely toned stomach, perky, natural breasts, and thick thighs that accentuated her big ass definitely complemented her pretty face. She felt empowered when she was nude. She laughed to herself, thinking of how she would someday save enough money to move to a nudist colony and spend the rest of her life naked, exposing her flawless body.

She brushed through her thick hair, untangling the raging ringlets. She continued singing to her reflection in the mirror. Her almond-shaped eyes, the color of honey, and thick, full lips reminded Niko just how much she resembled both her parents. She thought to herself how her Cuban uncles would always say to her, "You're so beautiful. You have the best of both worlds," as they would always admire her inherited beauty. She bounced into her bedroom closet, gliding to the beat of SZA's "Blind." She brushed her hair back into a neat bun and began rummaging through her closet, choosing a pair of black, fitted slacks, an ivory camisole, and a black, fitted, cropped blazer for her first day.

Niko knew she did not have to put forth much effort into being attractive. She had learned from one of the girls at the club how to go from the streets to the corporate if there was ever a need. Stacey was her name. She was a real down-to-earth Southern girl from Greenville, South Carolina. She was raised by two God-fearing, churchgoing parents and was taught to be very respectful of others. Stacey was accepted into UNC-Charlotte after graduating at the top of her high school class. However, in her sophomore year of college, Stacey found her means to an end by working alongside Niko as a stripper. She exuded an air of elegance in everything she did, and because of that, Niko looked up to her. Even the grimiest street niggas that patronized the strip club treated Stacey with respect, and her personality demanded it. During her senior year of college, she danced for the fun of it. Stacey would always advise Niko to get out at least before she turned 25 and reminded her that there was no way she should still be there by 30.

Stacey was smart when it came to business. She had shown Niko how she would always put away 10 percent of her earnings into something interest-bearing. She could hear Stacey's voice in the back of her head, *"You gotta be smart about your money. Remember, this kind of money comes fast, and it goes fast. Always prepare for that rainy day because it* will *come."* After Stacey graduated, she only danced that summer, and then she was gone. Niko lost touch with her and missed her dearly. Niko understood Stacey cutting ties with the club. She wasn't dancing to survive. She was dancing for fun. Besides, she did not want her secret to get out to her parents or sorority sisters. Niko considered looking up Stacey on Facebook, but that would only be after she established herself on this "real" job.

Niko slipped the slacks over her curvy size ten hips, then pulled the ivory cami over her head. She threw on her black heels from Aldo's that were very business casual and, most importantly, professional. She even kept her accessories classy. Niko didn't need much makeup, so she just added some mascara to her lashes and finished her look by coating her thick lips with her favorite lip gloss, Fenty Beauty Gloss Bomb. She looked in the mirror a final time before whispering, "Perfect," and then strolling about her day on the warm summer morning.

Niko was experiencing a case of the "first-day jitters" but reminded herself just why these jitters felt so good. She got in her car and tuned the radio to Power 98. This was the first day in a long time that she would be up early enough to catch No Limit Larry & The Morning Maddhouse on the radio. Listening to the radio helped to calm her nerves.

The commute was short. Before she knew it, she was pulling up to the three large buildings with the Charlotte Power sign in blue letters across the front. She drove around for what seemed like an hour, trying to find a parking space. Once she realized that she wouldn't find anything close to work, she settled on a parking lot about a quarter of a mile away. She growled as the thought of walking so far in the heat and heels began to consume her. She took off her blazer, grabbed her purse, and walked toward the building.

As the number 2801 became more visible to her, Niko stopped to put on her blazer. She took a deep breath, reached for the large glass door handle, and began to walk in. She sighed as the cool air hit her face. *Thank God for my Secret deodorant,* she thought, remembering she had a spare tube in her purse. A callback to her stripping days, always keeping something to ensure she was at her freshest.

"Please scan your badge, ma'am," the older white woman yelled without looking up from her computer monitor.

"Ooh, I'm sorry. It's my first day," Niko answered back. Suddenly, a foul odor hit her nostrils. It smelled like corn chips, onions, sweat, and some type of old food. She turned her head toward the smell and was greeted by a large, round belly.

"I got this, Amy," a voice exclaimed from a short distance.

A man began to approach her with a small Afro that was matted with pieces of lint in it. His face had patches of tightly coiled black and gray hair that were barely connected. Apparently, his hair did not grow enough to become a full beard or goatee. His shirt, which was more than likely once white, was now a dingy beige. His pants were two sizes too small and failed to reach the top of his shoes, which were leaning to the sides. Niko couldn't help but notice his ankles bulging from his dusty black shoes, resembling a busted pack of biscuits.

"How you doing today, young lady? My name is Darrell, but everyone calls me Big D," he said.

"I'm doing good, just ready to get my first day started," Niko answered with a smile that took everything inside her to muster up.

"Well, don't you worry, young lady. Big D will get you straight real quick, OK? You must be starting with the new training class today. Looks like you're the first to arrive. What's your name?"

Trying to hold her breath and respond at the same time, Niko answered, "It's Dominique Garcia."

"OK, Miss Garcia, for now, you can have a seat over there," he said, pointing to a row of chairs that lined the wide hallway to her left. "The rest of your group should be here soon. When everyone arrives, the trainer will take everyone to class."

Niko forced a smile onto her face and rushed over to a seat, happy to find relief from his hot and sour breath that was raging from his mouth.

Soon, the seats beside her began filling with others starting that day. As the others walked in, she looked into their faces, realizing these would be her new coworkers. After everyone signed in, Niko released a sigh of relief.

She was happy she didn't recognize any familiar faces in the group. She surely didn't want to see anyone from the club there. Most of the class was women, with only three men. Niko didn't know anyone else in the class; by the looks of things, no one else knew one another. Most were texting or playing games on their phones, seemingly uninterested in introducing themselves. Others stared in the distance while biting fingernails or bobbing their crossed legs anxiously.

The recruiter had previously explained to Niko that she would be in training for a couple of weeks before she would start taking calls, and that was just fine with her. Niko had mastered her communication skills in the streets, but she knew this would be a whole different ball game. She'd have to leave behind the ratchet vernacular she had become accustomed to using and become familiar with the use of proper English and good phone etiquette.

Just as Niko looked up from her phone, a tall, amber-skin-toned woman positioned herself at the top of the hall. Niko couldn't prevent her eyes from grazing the silhouette of her frame. She was floored by her beauty. The woman had long, black hair with sandy-brown highlights. She wore red-framed glasses that adorned her petite face and hazel eyes. Niko swallowed hard as she stared into the woman's eyes. The professional ensemble did very little to hide the curves that swelled at her bust and hips.

Working at the club for those years had given Niko a new appreciation for the female body. While she hadn't considered herself a lesbian or even bisexual in her youth, as an adult, her eyes had been opened to the sexual appeal and downright pleasures of being intimate with a woman. In Niko's eyes, no one was off-limits.

"Welcome to Charlotte Power and Light, otherwise known as CP and L," the woman greeted everyone, very poised. "I'm Erica, your trainer here at Charlotte Power. I hope everyone's ready to get started." A genuine smile lit up her face, accenting her high cheekbones. "All right, everyone, if you would please follow me." Everyone stood to follow Erica as she led the way toward the elevators. "I'm sure by now, everyone has met Big D," she mentioned with a dimming smile and raised eyebrow, looking in Big D's direction. Big D raised his hand, gesturing as if to say hello. "He'll help us get everyone's photos taken and your badges created later today." Niko couldn't help but notice subtle eye rolls and moans emanating from her fellow trainees. The thought of being in close quarters with Big D again made Niko's stomach turn.

Erica pressed the up arrow for the elevator while continuing her speech. "We're heading to the sixth floor. This is where you'll get your first look at where all the call center action takes place. Our training class isn't too far away from there, so get a good look while we're passing through. Just keep your voices down to avoid distracting the reps."

Erica led the way through a maze of pale gray cubicles on the sixth floor. She bobbed and weaved through the web of workstations until she led the group to a narrow hallway at the edge of the call center floor. Niko looked in amazement at everything around her like a tourist, as her new workplace looked nothing like the strip club where she once worked, not that she expected it to. She noticed the rectangular digital monitors that flashed numbers hanging from the ceilings. The hum of the many call-center employee's voices filled the air. She was both anxious and excited about the thought of having her very own cubicle. Most people had photos of their families, calendars, and office supplies at their workstations. Niko couldn't help but wonder if the images she wanted to display would be appropriate for this environment.

As the group entered the room, Niko had sudden flashbacks of high school. The classroom wasn't exactly what she remembered from high school, but there were obvious similarities. The room had five rows of desks with computers atop them. A wide center walkway split them into pairs on either side of the room.

"Feel free to pick your own seats," Erica instructed the group. "We're all adults here, so I don't think I need to go the path of assigning seats." Each desk had a name tent and a Sharpie. "Please use the Sharpie to write your name on the tent. You will use your name tent daily until we all become familiar with one another's names. Oh, and make sure that it's the name you prefer to be called. We'll be getting started soon with some brief introductions. Does anyone need to use the restroom before we get started?" Erica asked the class.

Niko quickly made her way to the front of the class, not because she needed to use the restroom but because this was the first time in her life that she ever wanted to be the teacher's pet. So, it was vital for her to get a seat at the front of the class. She glanced at the woman who'd taken the seat beside her, and it was apparent she had the same idea. She wrote the letters B-R-I-E-L-L-E on her tent card.

Brielle wore a modest button-up blouse with a gray skirt that hit just below her knees. The outfit was a total contrast to her cute baby face, making her age a complete mystery. Niko couldn't tell if she was an old lady with a young face or a young lady with a bad taste in clothing. However, that question was answered when the trainer led them in a round of introductions.

"OK, let's get started," Erica interrupted as everyone was getting situated at their desks, and some were still playing on their phones. "We can start at the back of the room and work our way up for introductions," Erica explained. "Please just tell us your name and a little bit about yourself, personally or professionally or both if you like."

One by one, each trainee gave details about themselves, giving Niko plenty of time to come up with something other than the truth about herself. Something told her that describing her years in the strip club wouldn't go far with her coworkers. And besides, she was starting a new life . . . ready to leave *most* of her past behind her. Of course, there were things like how Erica's hips bowed out from her narrow waistline that almost made her second-guess her new career choice. She was reminded that there were some aspects of her past that she simply could not and would not be able to relinquish. Certainly not now, and maybe not ever. She was actually intrigued and excited by the idea of blending some of those elements into her new life.

By the time it was Niko's turn, she had gleaned a few key corporate terms and phrases to make up a pretty believable background story. It was something short and sweet that didn't warrant many follow-up questions, in case someone wanted to ask a few.

"Hi, everyone. My name is Dominique, but I go by Niko. Um, I've worked in retail over the past few years," Niko explained, "and I wanted to use the skills I'd built during that time in a new arena. This just seemed like a good fit, you know, being able to combine both my people skills and sales experience." Niko ended with a pleasant smile that was matched with smiles from others across the room. Even Erica seemed pleased.

Niko's desk partner, Brielle, was the last to tell her story, "Hello, everybody," she said with a deep Southern drawl. "I'm pretty new to all of this. I've been at home caring for my little girl for the past year and a half. My husband and I decided it was a great time for me to reenter the workforce, and I'm ready to see what's in store for me here," she said eagerly.

Niko couldn't help but roll her eyes just a bit. She hated the type of woman who always had to insert the words "my husband" into every conversation. Before Niko had too much time to dwell on the imminent annoyance she was sure to be on its way to her new seatmate, Erica closed out the introductions with one of her own.

"Thank you, everyone, for sharing something from your background. We'll be spending a lot of time together over the next few weeks, so it's important that we get to know a little bit about one another. As for me, I've been with the company for over ten years now. I started in the same position just like you and eventually worked my way up to becoming a trainer. There are many great opportunities here, and this is a great department to start in because you'll learn a lot about the company in this particular position." Erica smiled, hoping that she had reassured everyone that they had made an excellent choice to come and work for the company.

The first part of the day was filled with a few online learning modules and a tour of the building. Before lunch, Erica escorted the group back to the lobby so they could have their images taken for their access badges. Big D seemed pleased at the sight of Niko again, but Niko glared with disgust as Big D smiled shamelessly with his brown, Cognac-stained teeth.

"Dom . . . Doma . . . Domaneeka," Big D stuttered, trying to pronounce her name.

"It's Dominique Garcia," Niko said, informing him of the correct pronunciation of her name.

"OK, Miss Garcia," he said in a sly tone, trying to flirt. "Take a seat here, and I'll get you all set up." He focused the camera on Niko. "Smile!" he shouted to Niko as if they were at the Picture People.

As Niko waited for her badge to print, she noticed that cliques had already begun to form amongst the group. Most people in the group paired with their desk mates, and some had a third person. As the room started to clear out, the only two people left were her and Brielle. Brielle took her seat on the stool while Big D took her picture. Just as he'd done to all of the other women in their group, Big D molested Brielle with his eyes monitoring closely every move she made.

Brielle smiled as she hurried beside Niko, trying to get away from him. She slightly shrugged her shoulders at Niko. "Hungry?"

"Yup," Niko replied, also ready to get away from Big D.

As he handed them their freshly printed badges, he began to speak. "Now when—" but before he could get his words out, they had already cleared the room. The two hurried out the front door, cutting short his opportunity to make small talk.

# Chapter 3

Niko and Brielle walked across the street to a strip mall with a few restaurants. They settled on a small soul food restaurant. As Niko watched Brielle eating her meal from across the table, she still couldn't figure out how she'd gotten stuck with her. Niko had never hung around "lames," and it was evident that Niko had also never hung around someone who was as square as Brielle seemed to be. Just then, she reminded herself, in the same way she'd been reminding herself all day, *This is a new beginning . . . have an open mind.*

"Sooo"—Niko started in-between bites—"how long have you been married?"

Brielle held up one finger while she finished chewing her food and wiping off crumbs from her mouth with a napkin. She placed the napkin back gently on her lap before responding. "Coming up on six years now."

"Really?" Niko exclaimed, "You don't look old enough to have been married that long."

"We met when we were kids, started dating at 15, got married at 18 . . ." She paused and shrugged. "The rest is history."

"Damn . . . That's a long time. I don't think I've ever had a boyfriend for longer than a year," Niko laughed, "and six months is even a stretch."

"Yeah, it's a long time to be with one person," Brielle continued. "We were both raised in the church, and so, you know . . ." She hesitated. "So, we got married so we could take our relationship to the next level . . . if you know what I mean." Brielle giggled like an innocent schoolgirl.

Niko couldn't help but think how different they were. The thought of being with only one man was utterly foreign to her. Not only could she not imagine it, but she also wasn't the least bit envious of that life. "Umph," Niko responded with a shrug. "I guess it's better not to know what you're missing than to be with someone and *know* that you could be getting better." Right then, Niko imagined Brielle having sex with a faceless man . . . missionary style, of course. She shook her head. *What a waste,* she thought. On their walk to the restaurant, Niko noticed that underneath all those modest clothes, Brielle seemed to have a cute figure with curves in all the right places.

Brielle interrupted Niko's thoughts. "Well, what about you? You got a boyfriend?"

Niko shook her head. "No, I don't really *do* boyfriends," she replied.

With a confused look on her face, Brielle asked, "Ooooh . . . so, you have a girlfriend?"

Niko laughed. "Let's just say relationships aren't my thing right now. I'm more of a free spirit when it comes to love. I don't like to limit myself."

"Ooh . . . OK," Brielle said. She was having difficulty wrapping her mind around that concept, so she did the one thing she knew how to do best. "I think you should come to church with me," she said with a wide smile.

Niko held back the urge to roll her eyes. She wasn't opposed to going to church but didn't want to go because someone was trying to "fix" her. From her perspective, Brielle could stand a bit of loosening up herself.

"Sure, I'll go. But if I go to church with you, you have to come out to a club with me one weekend."

"Wait, whaaaat?" Brielle responded incredulously, shaking her head before really considering the offer. There was no way her husband was going to go for that. "Uuuh, I don't know nothing about the club. I don't think I'm the club type."

"And why not? What are you afraid of? I mean, if your husband isn't going to allow it, I guess I do understand," Niko said with sarcasm in her tone.

Brielle's face got serious and indignant for a minute. "No, not at all. He doesn't control me or anything. I just try to respect our marriage by not going out and being tempted by the evil ways of the world. There's just so much temptation in the streets. And besides, I have nothing to wear. I'm just not the going-out type." It was apparent that Brielle was beginning to feel as if she had to justify herself and that she wouldn't do something so far out of her comfort zone for someone she had just met.

Niko quickly retorted, "And I've never been the church type, so I guess we are in the same boat." Niko extended her hand in an attempt to seal the deal with Brielle.

Brielle nodded and extended her hand apprehensively. "OK, well, I guess it's a deal. But no clubs where a lot of gangsters hang out," she requested sincerely.

"Deal!" Niko chuckled. "No gangsters."

# Chapter 4

A few more weeks of call center training passed. The entire training consisted of online learning modules, double-jacking phone lines to listen in on calls, and a few practice calls of their own. The last day of training finally arrived. Niko stood outside the elevator, waiting for it to make its way down to the lobby. Her five-inch beige stilettos were conservative but sexy, and her matching tote bag made the outfit corporate chic. As she checked her manicure, she saw a flash of light. She turned around to see Big D grinning at her, holding his phone.

"Whoo whee. Now, white is yo' color, girl. Yes, Lord!" Big D said, looking at his screen.

"I know you didn't just take a picture of my a—" Niko stopped herself. *This nigga is not about to pull me back into my old ways,* she thought. She had to handle this situation with tact and maturity. She gripped the strap of her tote tighter as her hand was itching to reach inside for her butterfly blade, but instead, she deeply inhaled, then exhaled as she thought about the professional environment she now worked in.

Quentin Martin walked up, and he could feel the tension between Big D and the females working there. "Good morning, good morning, good people," Quentin said, flashing a smile that would make a stampeding elephant stop and blush. He smiled at Niko and extended his hand. "You must be one of our new talented trainees. My name is Quentin, one of the team leads. You guys are coming to the production floor today, right?" he asked while making his presence known.

Niko smiled and nodded her head. Her eyes flashed back at Big D, only wishing she could strike his big, fat ass with lightning.

"What up, Q?" Big D said, holding his fist out for a dap. Quentin smiled and dapped his crusty knuckles.

"Nothing is up with me, Big D. What's up with you? I hope you're not bothering this young lady here."

"Nah, we just conversing is all, man. You know me, man, just chop'n it up. Trying to see how the new gig is going, ya know," Big D said, trying to pull the waistline of his pants over his bulging stomach.

"We were not *conversing* about anything," Niko interjected. "He took a picture of my butt."

Quentin turned to Big D, who was still displaying a big-ass smile. He winked at Quentin.

"D, c'mon now. You know you don't need any more complaints on you. Give me your phone, man." Quentin was always Big D's saving grace. He knew that Big D needed his job more than Big D realized that *he* needed his job.

"What, man? I'll delete it," Big D said with a disappointed look.

"D, give me your phone."

Big D mumbled and handed Quentin his phone. After a few moments, Quentin handed the phone back to him.

"Not cool, D. You really need to stop."

D snatched his phone and waddled back to the front desk.

"Thank you, sir," Niko said to Quentin as he pressed the up button for the elevator.

"Not a problem. You know, if you want to file a formal complaint, just say so, and I can report this to HR," Quentin said with an endearing Southern drawl.

Niko could tell that Quentin was one of those smooth Southern gentlemen, well-mannered and polite. He was also very handsome. Quentin wore glasses—a brown pair of Gucci frames, to be exact. He was garbed in a tailor-made tan suit, a melon-collared shirt underneath, and custom-colored Salvatore Ferragamo shoes on his feet. Although Niko was much more interested in the curves of a woman, Quentin's charm wooed her, leaving her crushing on him. He was nothing like the men she had met at the strip club. His smile was impeccable, and his genuine personality immediately relaxed her in his presence. She noticed his simple white gold Cartier Movado. Niko had a tiny obsession with watches. Most women judged men by their shoes, but she'd learned that a good timepiece tended to say much more about a man or, more importantly, how deep his pockets were.

Quentin glanced over to the other side of the elevator. He didn't notice a ring, but he did notice Ms. Dominique Garcia looked very young. He took in the young woman's thick, black hair, full lips, and tight body. Yeah, she was definitely going to be trouble around the office, and he couldn't wait to see what the fellas had to say once they got a look at Charlotte Power & Light's newest bombshell.

They arrived at the sixth floor, and Niko stepped off the elevator first. Quentin couldn't help but notice this girl had that "catwalk swagger," like she walked to her own soundtrack. *And damn, dem white pants.* Quentin's thoughts wandered as he leaned his head to one side. It wasn't that her ass was huge. She was just so damn sexy. After getting a closer look as he walked behind her, Quentin could hardly blame Big D. The view was mesmerizing.

Niko paused midstep, snapping Quentin back to reality. "So, do you know who Ms. Cummings is? I was told that she would be my manager," Niko inquired. She wished he could be her manager as fine as he was, but instead, she and Brielle had been assigned to Ms. Cummings's team. She just hoped that Ms. Cummings would be just as cool. Niko planned to find out today and hopefully report back to Brielle, who wasn't set to start on the floor until the following day. Niko wished it was the other way around so she would know what to expect.

"Oh, yeah. That's my girl. She's one of the best team leads on the floor. Well, outside of myself," Quentin responded while adjusting his suit jacket.

Niko smiled and unconsciously began biting her bottom lip. She prayed that some of her classmates would show up and ease her nerves.

"But look, let's put your things down, and I'll introduce you to the crew. Ms. Cummings's team is just three rows over, but she doesn't normally make it in 'til 'bout nine thirty or ten on Mondays. So, we got some time to show you around a little." Quentin led the way to his desk and unlocked the overhead compartment of the first cubicle. He put his laptop bag inside. "You can put your things in here until we figure out where Tiff's gonna sit you."

"OK, cool . . ." Niko checked herself. "I mean . . . What I meant to say was thank you . . . Thank you, Mr. . . . . Oh jeez, I'm so sorry." She was so comfortable with him that slang just rolled off her tongue like she had known him forever.

Quentin laughed as Niko tried to gather her thoughts. "Niko, just call me Q. Besides, everyone around here calls me Q for short. You're officially part of the team now, so you're good."

She was so relieved that she'd beaten her new boss to the office, but she didn't want to appear too relaxed already. She smiled nervously and placed her bag in the overhead compartment. Quentin locked the door and led her toward the break room. "Hey, you can loosen up a little. Trust me, it's cool. We keep it pretty casual around here." Quentin smiled, and Niko was definitely appreciative of the gesture.

"You drink coffee, or would you like some juice or something?" Q asked, offering her a morning beverage or snack. The lounge area was always known to have complimentary food and drinks for the staff.

"I'm OK. I think I'm just a little nervous. You know, this is my first 'official' day on the floor." Niko felt compelled to be honest with him.

"Well, take it from me, Dominique, don't be. You'll be great and have all of this mastered in no time." Q was doing everything in his power to help Niko feel at ease.

"Sounds good . . . And please, Q, call me Niko," she invited. "Mrs. Garcia is my mother, and my dad only calls me Dominique when he's angry . . . Soooo, if you want me to call you Q, then please, just call me Niko."

"A'ight then, Miss Niko. I got ya." Quentin smiled and opened the break room door.

"'Sup, my dude?" a tall, lanky, light-skinned brother said before noticing the woman Quentin had with him. He turned and leaned against the counter, shaking up a protein shake. He began sizing up the new girl as the pair walked toward the snack counter in the break room. He smiled. "Oh, pardon me. Good morning, Ms. . . ." he said, extending his free hand.

"Just call me Niko." She smiled. This was no doubt the second of many introductions today. "Pleasure."

"Niko, this is Sean Powell, another of Tiffany's and my counterparts." Quentin made the introductions.

"The pleasure is mine." Sean was taken aback by the new girl's face. She was so fine he couldn't help the flirtatious smile on his face. But more than that, he couldn't help but wonder where he'd seen this woman before. He couldn't place the face but couldn't ignore that walk and how she was wearing those cuffed ivory slacks. He decided to dismiss the thought as déjà vu. "Welcome to CP and L, young lady."

Sean shot a glance at Quentin—all but saying what they both knew. *Damond is gon' have a field day with this one.* Quentin immediately knew what Sean was thinking and reached to give him a pound. Both guys had found it entertaining to watch their boy Damond prey, pounce, and then discard the many wounded women of CP&L. They lived vicariously through his exploits, and Niko was clearly going to be his next victim.

Niko, unaware of the whole silent exchange, gazed up at the TV screen mounted in the break room. CNN was playing the latest news spin, and she pretended to be interested. She sat at one of the multicolored break room tables and crossed her legs under the near-hypnotized gaze of the two men behind her. Quentin cursed those white pants for the third time, and Sean just shook his head.

Even when Niko didn't try, her stride was seductive. Seduction had always come so naturally that she'd learned to use it to her advantage early in life. Stripping had come easy to her because of those subtle, sexual nuances—like her walk. But after a few short years, stripping on a stage had stopped feeling empowering to her. Girls getting strung out, beaten, or raped by psychos who thought they owned them . . . and some getting turned over to the streets when they were too worn out for the stage—or even worse. Niko knew there was more to life for her. After four long years, she was out of the game and starting over, and she considered CP&L her stage now. Her mother had always told her women had an innate ability to command the very air in a room with the right walk, right attitude, and right game. This little mundane office would be no different, she thought as she looked around. *This place could use some swag.* Niko sneakily smiled to herself.

"So, Ms. *Just* Niko." Sean broke the ice. "You're gonna be on Tiffany's team, eh? Good team. The sharpest bunch here if you ask me. I don't know what she's been doing, but Tiff's been top dawg all year."

"That's fantastic. I can't wait to meet her." Just as Niko spoke, the break room door swung open, and two women walked in.

"Good Monday, Angie. Hey, Jena." Quentin announced the women, more than just greeting them.

"Hello, Quentin, Sean." Angie nodded as she walked toward the coffeemaker. Angie was tall with beautiful copper-brown, flawless skin. Her hair was pulled back into a high bun on the top of her head. She didn't wear much makeup, but she also didn't need it. Her naturally high cheekbones and slanted eyes offered her face more than you could buy at a MAC counter. Niko couldn't help but notice how attractive she was, but the energy she gave off was the complete opposite. God had blessed Angie with big breasts and a big ass, but clearly, judging by the choice of outfit she had worn that day, she struggled with deciphering between club wear and corporate wear. *Sometimes, women just don't know how to work what God gave 'em,* Niko thought to herself . . . *and this female is proof of that.*

Angie was ranting to Jena as she busied herself over the sink, rinsing her coffee mug. Something about someone parking in her spot and how she worked too damn hard for security not to do their job and regulate parking.

Niko spoke first. "Good morning, ladies. I'm Niko Garcia. It's nice to meet you."

Angie paused with somewhat of a frown on her face. The look was as if Niko had very rudely interrupted her rant. Jena smiled.

Niko grinned and casually dismissed the disgruntled broad, turning to the smiling Jena.

"Well, you're a new fresh face this Monday morning," Jena answered in the cutest voice. "Nice to meet you too. First day?"

Jena was much shorter and much thicker than Angie. Her hair was cut in a sharp bob with Chinese bangs. She was a doll baby, Niko thought. She always sized women up by how they would fit in her former life at the club. Jena looked to Niko like she could have been something like a showstopper. Her body was a ten, but she wasn't as much a natural beauty. Jena was cute, and she had that bowleg walk that men loved. Niko shot Jena a coy grin almost out of habit. Niko smiled to herself. *Bad habits die hard,* she thought as she shook her head.

"Yeah, first-day jitters, I suppose." Niko masked her thoughts.

"Oh, girl, don't worry about it. Ain't nothing to it . . . I mean, brain surgery it's not, even when people wanna make it seem like it's a matter of national security," Angie said. Jena, Quentin, and Sean simultaneously shot Angie a glance at the remark. "Just remember, it's a call center. Just smile and dial, even when you don't feel like it . . . But you'll be fine."

Jena seemed cool. She spoke in a Gullah dialect, like someone from the low country in South Carolina.

"Well, that's good to know. And thanks." Niko's nerves appreciated the advice. "So far, I'm just getting familiar with everyone. Quentin . . . Sean . . . and now you." Niko smiled at the China doll while again ignoring Angie's obnoxious attitude and too-small red suit. "What's the accent?" Niko noticed everyone watching the special attention she seemed to be paying Jena as Jena joined her at the table.

Quentin and Sean suddenly felt invisible. Eyebrows raised, they thought, *What the hell just happened?* Women were usually a lot of fun to watch, but was it possible that these women were flirting right in front of them?

"I'm from Charleston." Jena sipped her green tea. "I came here for school a couple of years ago, but then I had my son and had to work. I took a few retail jobs and came to CP and L 'bout a year ago. It's cool. I plan on going back to school in the fall, though. Well, once I get my son's day care straight."

"I know the feeling," Niko agreed, then caught herself. "Well, not the day care thing, but finishing school. I need to get on that myself."

Angie rudely interrupted. "Tell me they're not hiring people who barely got outta high school now . . . Wow." She scoffed loudly enough to remind everyone she was still in the room.

*What the hell did you say?* Niko thought to herself as her eyes darted from the TV to the too-small red suit. Angie kept her back to the group while putting cream in her coffee. Niko could already tell that this bitch was going to be a problem.

Sean chimed in, half-laughing, half-clearing his throat. "So, err uh, Niko. You from the QC?" Her accent and demeanor didn't sound like anyone from the South he'd ever met. He was still trying to place that face.

"Well, I'm somewhat of an army brat, kinda from everywhere. My family settled in NC about ten years ago, though, and I've been here ever since. What about you?" Niko kept it vague. She knew to keep her personal life personal, which was her rule at any job.

"Oh, I'm Charlotte-born and bred, sis." Sean laughed. "A product of West Meck High, JCSU, and now CP and L for the last five years . . . surrounded by all the Queen

City queens I can stand." He shared another pound with Quentin. "Shiiiit, this is home for me, and ain't no place like it," Sean said proudly.

"Language!" Angie looked over at Sean to remind him that he was in a place of business.

"Chill, Ang. I left my mother's house years ago."

Angie hurried out of the room, mumbling about why corporate doesn't just place a "Now Hiring" sign in the window.

"What the hell was that?" Niko couldn't help but laugh.

"*That* was Angie Tisdale, girl. Don't pay her *no* 'tention. She loves to say shit to piss people off 'cause otherwise, nobody would even acknowledge her." Jena wafted Angie's presence away like an invisible gnat.

"So, where were you going to school? Was it here in Charlotte?"

Niko wanted to answer honestly and say, "Hard Knock University," but she laughed off the thought. "I haven't enrolled yet. Classrooms were always so confining for me, so I think I'll pick up a few online classes this year."

The break room door flew open again. "Wassup, Black people?" A new voice entered the break room, a metallic pink coffee mug in hand. He yawned. "Ugh, why y'all in here all cackling like hens n'shit? Did that bitch Angie get hit by a bus like I dreamt last night?"

All at once, the whole room erupted in laughter. The timing of this new character was impeccable.

"For real! I did. I really dreamt that shit."

"Torry, you going to hell." Sean tried not to laugh but couldn't help it.

"Torry, meet Niko." Jena managed an introduction through tears as she laughed.

Torry made no secret of how much he couldn't stand Angie Tisdale. He was also very funny with his flamboyant personality.

"Hello." Niko looked over at Torry and smiled.

Torry stood slender at about six foot three and almost vogued with every motion as he walked. His ensemble was faultless. He rocked a pair of tapered eggshell-white Express slacks with a fitted gray V-neck. Torry's thin waist was a perfect match for his Louis Vuitton black belt that coordinated with his Louis Vuitton charcoal-gray loafers. His D&G shades hugged the face of his little pea head. He looked more like a European runway model than a call center jockey.

"Well, hello, pretty girl," Torry politely exclaimed, lifting his shades up just past his crisp hairline to get a better head-to-toe look. "Love the peep toe, boo. Bebe's?"

"Close. Baker's clearance rack, hon." Niko stuck out her foot to expose her shoe game.

"Ballin' on a budget. I know that shit." Torry replaced the shades on his face. "'Bout time y'all got something as pretty as me up in this bitch." His hips swished as he searched the cabinets, slamming each cabinet door of the kitchenette. "I know y'all better not have drank up my Colombian roast . . . or I'm tossing one of y'all mofos under a bus for real. I *know* I had some left last week." He worked his way to the cabinets behind where Quentin and Sean were posted up. He faked a smile. "Hey, fellas. *Excuse* me."

"Heeeey, Torry," the fellas said in a synchronized tone.

"How 'bout y'all kindly move y'all pretty asses out of my way before I snap? Thank youuuu."

The guys just laughed and separated so Torry could open the doors. There on the top shelf was his Colombian roast.

"See, y'all playing games." Torry popped the lid to see how much coffee he had left. "Y'all better be glad we got company today. Lawd Jesus, y'all finna work my nerves early this morning." Torry turned his attention back to Niko. "So, pretty girl, have they told you your team yet?"

Quentin answered for her. "She's gonna be with Ms. Cummings's Customer Service Rep Team."

"Oh. Tiffany? That's my baby right there. She is so sweet. You gon' love her," Torry said excitedly while waiting for his coffee to percolate. As the coffee machine began to make that familiar sound, Torry began to chant and gyrate. "Uh-oh. It's time for the percolator. It's time for the percolator . . ."

"You so stupid, Torry. Stop trippin' in front of company. You worse than them two-dollar hoes at Onyx." Jena couldn't stop laughing.

Suddenly, with that statement, Sean remembered where he knew Niko from. He nearly choked on his protein shake. Damond wasn't gonna believe this shit. "Well, good people, I'm 'bout to get my day started. And, Ms. Niko . . ." Sean walked around to face her to get a good look and be sure he wasn't wrong. "Hope your first day goes great. Let me know if there is anything I can do to help you." He thought it funny that she didn't seem to recognize him and couldn't help but wonder if she would recognize Damond. "I just sit one row away from Tiff."

Torry was still clapping and singing in the background as he prepared his coffee. "Bah ba da bah bah . . . bah ba da bah bah . . ."

"Thank you, Sean." Niko couldn't help but begin to feel welcomed.

"A'ight. Cool. Hey, y'all have a good day as well." Sean almost tripped over a chair, rushing out of the room.

Torry was finally done, and so was his coffee. "Must you do that every morning?" Quentin thought it was a reasonable question.

"Just for special occasions. Y'all were boring this pretty thang to death." Torry winked at Niko. "I just wanted to make sure she knew we weren't all corpses in this piece."

The door swung open again. Angie stood framed in the threshold. "Um, Jena, I'm sure you won't need a break today since you've taken all this personal time so early in the day. We have calls in queue, and there are some metric reports from last week that we need to go over. Soooo . . . when you're done here . . ." She disappeared as abruptly as she had appeared.

"G'lawd have mercy! I cannot stand that bitch!" Torry snapped. "Was that camel toe I smelled broiling in those tight-ass pants? Uuugh, I thought she was on Weight Watchers or something. And ain't nobody trying to scc her nasty-ass camel-toe shit! A bitch need to let that shit breathe. Maybe if she gave the pussy some air, that ass wouldn't be so damn uptight."

Niko, Quentin, and Jena laughed.

"Is she always like that?" Niko asked but already knew the answer from how everyone reacted to Angie.

"Oh, you haven't seen the half of it. She was nice today . . ." Jena warned. "But like we said, don't pay her no mind. If she messes with you, just let me know." Jena wasn't sure why she'd said that, except that she seemed to instantly like Niko. "Y'all have a good day." Jena snuck a final glance at Niko and rushed out the door.

Torry just shook his head as he sipped his steaming hot Colombian roast from his metallic pink mug. Then he vented, "That arrogant hooker is the worst! She got that little sideways promotion, making the same as Quentin and them, but she wanna be a 'senior.' Bitch, please." He blew his coffee before taking another sip. "Don't let her stress you, chile. You see these worry lines?" He pointed out his forehead to Niko. "Shit, I looked as pretty as you when I started here. Now look at me."

"Baby, you are nothing short of fabulous." Niko smiled, admiring Torry and his bluntness. She already knew she loved him.

"Well, Miss Niko, let's see if your boss lady's gotten in yet. She can set you up in your cube and get you going." Quentin groaned as he stood up like an old man getting up from a nap.

"Damn, Q. I forgot you was back there eavesdropping. You betta make yo'self known fo' something happen, chile. You know I was in the war, honey. Ooooh Lord, my nerves . . ." Torry fanned invisible vapors.

"A'ight, Torry, we gonna do lunch before the week is out, all right?" Niko winked at him.

"Oh, fuh sho, baby girl. And I'ma be by to check on you later . . . I need to bring my girl Avery by to meet you anyway. She gonna love your little cute ass."

"Dat's wassup." Niko was already comfortable with Torry. They shared a double-cheek air kiss as Niko made her way out the door.

Quentin was holding the door as Niko walked through it. "Torry, man, *try* to stay out of trouble today. It's only Monday." Quentin grinned.

"If that's how you want it, *man*," Torry mocked, placing a huge piece of coffee cake in his mouth.

Quentin just shook his head and walked out to the floor. Niko stood patiently, waiting for him to catch up. Her head still spun from everyone she was meeting, and it wasn't over.

The sales floor was abuzz already with all the reps on calls. The phones were ringing off the hook.

"Nine calls in queue. Four hang-ups already, people. Somebody pick up the phone." Niko could hear Angie's agitated voice yelling. Quentin pointed to a black screen mounted from the ceiling with a ticker scrolling across red letters.

"See that? That's how we measure our productivity in this office compared to other offices nationwide. People like Sean look at that to measure what everyone is doing every minute of the day." Quentin wondered to himself what had made Sean rush out like he did.

Niko walked with her hands in her pockets, nodding as Quentin pointed out the different offices, teams, and departments on the floor. She pretended to understand everything he said as he explained each area's function and what each team was in place to do. In reality, she was glad she was walking because the information would otherwise put her to sleep. She was still adjusting to these working mornings.

Quentin looked at his watch. He knew his 10:30 meeting was fast approaching, and he'd not been at his desk all morning. He led Niko over to see if Tiffany had gotten in yet. "I'm not really sure which seat will be yours, but let's get you some manuals on the phone operations to read through while I get ready for my meeting this morning."

They turned onto the row where her team would be and heard a woman's voice ending a phone call. "OK, honey. Mommy has to get to work. Call me when you get home from school, OK? Love you. Have a great day."

"Ah, yes, and this sounds like your lovely boss lady, Ms. Cummings," Quentin said as he approached Tiffany's workspace.

Tiffany Cummings hung up her call and swiveled her desk chair around. "Well, good morning, Mr. Combs. How are you?"

"Doing just fine, lady. Great to finally see ya." Quentin thinly masked his sarcasm. "Just showing your newest recruit around a little. I wasn't sure where you'd designated her cube to be. But anyway, Niko Garcia, this is Tiffany Cummings, your team's lead." Quentin smiled.

"Nice to finally meet you, Dominique. Or is it Niko?" Tiffany shook Niko's hand.

Niko could barely find her voice. She couldn't believe that she was still nervous. "Um, oh, it's Niko. I mean, I-I'm Niko. Nice to meet you as well."

Tiffany was a strikingly beautiful woman with long, sandy-brown hair pulled back in a plain ponytail. Her skin was flawless; not a blemish in sight. Her eyes were emerald green. Looking into them, you could almost see into her soul. She wore a tan skirt and a pink blouse complemented by an oversized scarf draped around her neck.

"So . . . Mr. Quentin hasn't been boring you too badly, has he?" Tiffany laughed and nudged Quentin's arm a little.

"Oh, no, ma'am, I haven't been bored at all. Just meeting everyone. Getting acquainted with some of the other reps and managers. Seems like a fun bunch," Niko said, trying to play it cool.

"Yeah, just kept it basic, Tiff," Quentin added.

"We'll take it from here." Tiffany looked over at Quentin, confirming she was ready to start her day.

"Cool . . . And, Tiff, we got a ten thirty with Rizzo this morning. Don't be late for *that*."

"Gotcha." Tiffany loved how Quentin could always be depended on to keep her head in the game around here. He was a lifesaver. "See you in a bit."

Niko sat down. Tiffany turned and sat down in her desk chair.

"So, Ms. Niko, let me officially welcome you to CP and L. I'll be your manager, supervisor, coach, whatever you want me to be to make us a successful team. If you have any concerns, please let me know. I'm here to help you." Tiffany was hoping to make Niko feel a little more comfortable.

The two women chatted about how Niko's morning had been so far. Tiffany seemed to be listening while she searched her cube for the materials she would need for her meeting in about half an hour.

Niko tried to focus, talking about the characters she'd met so far and what Quentin had shown her about each team's function on the floor. She watched her new boss lean, crawl, and stretch around the small space, reaching under where Niko was sitting. Tiff then reached above Niko's head in search of meeting materials.

"Torry's a trip, huh?" Tiffany spoke while she relaxed for a moment. "I love that he keeps it lively around here. Every now and then, I have to get him to bring it down to about a five because he's *always* at ten." She laughed.

"Yeah, he's something else. I can tell. I think we'll be quick friends. And, um, can I help you find what you're looking for?" Niko said while standing up.

"Oh, girl, no. Sit. Sit. It's just Monday, and I have this meeting I forgot about, and I can't remember . . ." Tiffany paused as if suddenly she remembered what exactly she was looking for. She crouched down to look in a drawer with her back to Niko. She continued to say under her breath that she wouldn't remember where her head was if it wasn't attached. Niko smiled.

Tiffany's blouse lifted, and Niko noticed what looked like a birthmark on the small of Tiffany's back. For some reason, the mark was reminiscent of one Niko had seen before. Niko stood and reached for the Kleenex box on Tiffany's desk without taking her eyes off the strawberry-shaped mark just above Tiffany's waistline. She accidentally knocked over several framed pictures and pencil holders with about a hundred pens and highlighters. "Oh God, I'm so sorry." Niko was never this nervous. "I'm not usually clumsy, I promise." She rushed to gather the items.

"Oh, it's fine, sweetie." Tiffany reached over to help Niko put the pencils back. "This desk is a mess anyway. I need to clean it, but my goodness, I never have time."

While picking up the pens, Tiffany noticed her hands were ashy. She picked up a tube of Japanese cherry blossom lotion and poured some into her hands. "Uugh, I hate when that happens." She'd squeezed too much, so she took Niko's hands. "Here, take some of this," she said as she rubbed the lotion into Niko's hands.

She could see her newest hire seemed nervous on her first day, and she remembered how nervous she had been when she had started. She decided to take a moment with Niko before her meeting, not for training, but just to put her at ease.

"Don't worry about this. I'll get it later when I clean up the rest of this stuff. Listen . . ." Tiffany patted the lotion onto Niko's petite hands. "I should apologize. This is no way to start a new job. I know it's nerve-racking enough on your first day, and it doesn't help that I'm sort of all over the place today. So, let's start this way," Tiffany continued. "I have this theory that the more I know about my people, the more we can create a cohesive team and propel each other's successes in this company. You shine, I shine. Make sense?"

Niko nodded.

"So, tell me something about yourself." Tiffany wasn't particularly interested in learning Niko's life story right then. She just wanted to break the ice and help to relax her.

"Well . . ." Somehow, Niko wasn't prepared for that question. "I'm very excited about starting here today. I haven't really worked at a place like this before, but I'm a fast learner. And I live for a challenge. So . . ."

Tiffany grinned. "OK, OK. So, now answer the same question without quoting your résumé. I've already read that."

Niko felt herself blush and bit her lower lip. She was speechless.

"I mean, my team has a good time, and we work well with each other because we all get along. We know each other very well, and we support each other. Like a little family. So, tell me about Niko Garcia."

Niko could barely focus. She'd heard Tiffany speaking, but her heart was pounding so loud she couldn't think. Having a past life like hers didn't allow her to start off being honest with people, no matter how nice they seemed. Niko decided once she found her voice, she'd be honest but abstract.

"I'm a bit complicated. I love to laugh, and I can keep a secret. I don't mind a calm walk on the beach, but I'd rather jump into the middle of a big wave. People like to see me dance, but I dance best when I'm alone, and I write poetry. That's my way of saying all the things that would probably get me in trouble if I said them out loud." Niko sighed and started to feel at ease.

"OK-K-K." Tiffany laughed. "That's fantastic. I like poetry too. And actually, Tate—one of your teammates— even does a little spoken word, I'm told. And, girl, you will love Tate. Actually, all the ladies do. Well, except me, of course," she digressed. "I'm something of a one-man woman."

Somehow, that last point didn't come across as if Tiffany *liked* being a "one-man woman," she thought.

"So, this is great!" Tiffany changed gears a little but with the same energy. "Now that we've gotten a little more acquainted, I'm gonna sit you with Tate for a while. You can shadow him and watch how things work around here while I check out what they're discussing in this meeting." Tiffany closed her desk drawer and stood up.

"Make sure you ask Tate plenty of questions. He's one of my best go-to people around here, and I wanna make sure you have a good understanding of how the team works. Plus, he can introduce you to the rest of the team while I'm gone. Cool?"

"Will I shadow you at all?" Niko hated having so little time with her new boss, but she tried hard not to sound like she'd been completely spoiled already.

"Of course you will, sweetie. I won't throw you to the wolves just yet." Tiffany winked playfully.

She led Niko to a cube a few units down, where a white guy sat. He was tall and solid and wore slightly oversized khakis that sagged slightly with a yellow Ralph Lauren Polo knit top.

"Good morning, Tate." Tiffany surprised Tate, who was leaning in his chair with this headset on and scribbling on a notepad.

"Good morning, Tiff. What's good this Monday morning?"

"This is your newest teammate, Niko Garcia. Niko, meet Tate."

Niko smiled at the Paul Walker look-alike. "Hello, Tate."

"Tate, I need you to show our new girl the ropes and introduce her to the team. I got a meeting with Rizzo in about five minutes. You cool with that?"

"You know I got whatever you need, boss lady. She's in great hands." Tate's swagger was so honest that Niko could immediately see why Tiffany said all the women swooned for him. Black women love their Jon B. types.

Niko didn't swoon for Tate like most would expect. However, she did find him highly attractive, even if he wasn't quite her type.

"Perfect. I shouldn't be more than an hour or so." Tiffany's voice trailed off as she sped down the aisle toward the elevators.

"So, Miss Niko Garcia." Tate smiled. "Welcome to CP and L."

# Chapter 5

Tiffany arrived at the meeting just as the clock reached 10:30. She chose the only available seat between Erica and Damond.

"Love the suit. Is it new?" Damond loudly whispered at Tiffany.

She faked a smile but kept her back to him as if he'd said nothing.

He took a notable, deep breath and exhaled. "Damn, girl. You even smell nice too." Damond was incessant.

"Shhhh!" Erica didn't mask her annoyance well.

Damond tapped his left hand lightly on the long, cherrywood table designated for board meetings. Twirling his wedding band with his thumb, he tapped the table again to hear the sound of the metal against the wood. T*ap, tap*. It stirred everyone's attention away from the coordinator of the meeting, but more than anything, it was Damond's way of showing how mundane these Monday morning meetings had become to him.

"Oh, sorry. Excuse me," he'd say to everyone, every meeting, every time the "tap" got distracting. Damond was the head manager of the entire call center. Not only was he in charge, but he was also well connected to the owner, who was his college roommate. Damond had attended the predominantly white North Carolina State University. Although he only played basketball for two years, he was extremely popular on campus. Damond had conquered the few attractive Black girls attending the university within the first year, so he began his conquest of the European ladies the following year. By the time he had graduated, Damond had nearly tasted every ethnicity on the campus. And indeed, what he might have missed from his college days, he had well made up during his time at CP&L. Being head manager allowed him to do as he pleased within the call center, which was 90 percent female and only 10 percent male employees. The company had a turnover rate of over 50 percent, which also meant the numbers for him having something new to play with monthly was surely in his favor. He had never thought that the job would be so rewarding when his old college buddy proposed he run the place. But it had clearly become the best and worst decision of his life. Best, of course, to fulfill his never-ending thirst, but worst in the fact that he was a married man with a family. As he sat there bored, he could only think and hope that the new hiring for the service blizzard would produce new prospects.

Almost as if he were reading Damond's mind, Sean, who sat to his right side, had written a note that would surely garner his attention. He slid the paper under Damond's left hand as he attempted to make the "tap" sound again.

*An old friend has found her way back to you, old man. A bit more clothing this time . . . This time, wearing the shit outta some white pants. But I'd know that ass anywhere, and it's seated on Tiffany's team. She looks just as good as the last time we saw her . . . at your bachelor's party. Nigga, the world just got a little smaller.*

Damond turned toward Sean and mouthed, "The fuck you mean? *She's here?*"

As soon as the meeting ended, Damond and Sean entered Damond's office.

"So, you telling me *she's* here? And on Tiff's team?" Damond was so excited he could barely keep it together.

"Uh-huh," Sean said, smiling.

Damond placed his phone in his top drawer and dapped Sean.

"Well, I guess it's time I reintroduce myself," Damond added.

He and Sean walked down the hall toward the call center rooms. As they turned the corner, the sounds of voices on phones hummed. It was 12:30 p.m., and the first wave having lunch was coming back to their desks as others were preparing to go. Sean scanned the floor. He spotted Tiffany at her desk and Niko seated beside her. He knew that this was going to be worth the price for admission once Damond and ole girl reconnected.

Niko was sitting with her legs crossed, while Tiffany was on her desk, trying to reach something on the top shelf. Her skirt had risen, and her creamy cocoa thighs were exposed as she struggled to reach the files.

"Do you need some help, Ms. Cummings?" Niko couldn't help but ask, possibly getting a chance to be closer to Tiffany to get a better view of her toned, beautiful thighs.

"No, you sit right there, doll. I got it," Tiffany responded as she grabbed the green file folder. "Oh, I don't know why I put that up there," she added, nearly out of breath as she climbed down from her desk. She adjusted her skirt and smoothed back her hair.

"Well, Tiffany, I must say that I enjoyed seeing you move like that," Sean said, smiling.

"Sean, Damond. Hey, guys. Whatcha need?" Tiffany asked, ignoring his comment.

"We good, but have you seen Quentin? We were about to grab some lunch," Damond asked.

"No, no, I haven't seen him. Well, not since earlier. I've been getting Ms. Niko here an introduction to the team, and she's already started off with a bang. Tate says she's going to be his competition. Niko, I think you met Sean this morning, and this is Damond Wilks. He's the head of the call center."

Niko turned around and smiled at Damond.

"Hello," she said, barely making eye contact with either of them.

Damond felt the air leave his lungs, and his throat became dry when he looked into Niko's eyes.

"Ms. Cumming, would you mind if I went to the restroom?" Niko asked as she stood.

"No, not at all. Do you know where it is?" Ms. Cummings asked, pointing in the direction of the ladies' room.

Niko stepped between Sean and Damond. "Excuse me . Oh, it was nice to meet you, Mr. Wilks."

Damond stared as she walked up the aisle. He watched her hips sway, noticing that nothing had changed about her. Even in *those* clothes, she still walked with the stealth of a sleek panther.

His shock turned to disappointment as he realized Niko had walked by him like she didn't know him. As a matter of fact, she had damn near looked straight *through* him.

"OK. Well, Tiff, we gonna see if Quentin is back at his desk," Sean said, pushing Damond's shoulder. Damond stood still, watching Niko until she disappeared around the corner.

# Chapter 6

Niko walked past Angie as she entered the restroom. She refused to make eye contact with her because she was not interested in dealing with Angie's negativity. Niko looked in the mirror, thinking, *Is this what I really want to do?* She turned the water on, thinking she should splash some of it on her face. Just then, someone was coming out of one of the stalls. Niko didn't look up at first because she was replaying the thought of Ms. Cummings's thighs in her head and didn't want any distractions. She leaned over to splash water on her face when she heard a familiar voice say, "Treasure?"

Niko closed her eyes, leaning her head back, realizing it had to be someone from the strip club. Treasure was the stage name that she went by when she danced. No way would anyone there know that unless they had cashed her out at some point. Scared to look up, Niko also recalled the familiarity in the voice that had just exposed her previous life.

"It's me, boo . . . Rho. Damn, let me find out you done traded in the strip pole for a headset. What yo' fine ass doin' up in here?" Rho asked jokingly.

Rhonda was her name, but those who knew her from the streets called her Rho, and she was a blast from Niko's past. At one time, Rho was Niko's biggest fan and also one of her most loyal, well-paying clients during her stripping days.

Niko turned around. "What the fuck are you doing here, Rho? Don't tell me you work here too." Niko couldn't believe her eyes. She was excited and embarrassed all at the same time.

Of all the places in the world, she did not expect to see Rho working in a call center. She never carried herself like someone who would even consider working in the corporate world. She was an around-the-way hustler from what Niko knew about her. Rho *lived the life,* being well known as one of the biggest dope dealers in Charlotte. Rho was a regular at the strip club and was known to make it rain on Niko for her skilled ability to make her ass jiggle, amongst other things. It was evident that Rho had the same idea as Niko, wanting a change of pace, and decided to leave the street life for something a little more stable.

"Ayo, so, like you work here n'shit?" Rho was so happy to run into Niko, and it was written all over her face. "Let me get your number, shorty." She asked, hoping to catch up in more ways than one. She recalled from back in the day how Niko had this one rule: never mix business with pleasure. She assumed that if she had managed to get Niko to bend the rule back in the day, then maybe there was a chance she would do it again. Even better, she hoped the rule no longer existed, and Niko would recall the times Rho pleased her by *giving her the business.*

Rhonda was a gorgeous lesbian who preferred to display the look of a more dominating appearance. Niko couldn't help but blush. She was flattered that Rho was still crushing on her after all this time. She went into a quick daze, remembering the nights she spent with Rho's head buried deep between her thighs as she tugged at her long, soft, well-groomed locs. She recalled the gentle but firm licks of Rho's tongue across her swollen clit. One thing Niko knew for sure and that was Rho had mastered the art of eating pussy.

Niko quickly snapped out of it at the sound of Rho's voice trying to get her to agree to give up her contact information. After the scene that had just jogged Niko's memory, she would be a fool not to give Rho her number.

"OK, cool. I'll give you the number," Niko said with a sneaky smirk on her face. "But in the meantime, let's keep this under wraps. I'm new here and don't need people in my business already." Niko pulled a paper towel from the dispenser and took the pen from behind Rho's ear to write down her number. She handed Rho the paper, then gestured with her finger to her lips as if to say, *"Ssssh, don't tell."* Niko turned to exit the restroom, and Rho watched as her phat ass disappeared out the door.

"Damond, Damond?" Tiffany said, laughing. Damond realized his mouth was open. He tried to swallow, but his mouth was dry. "Are you okay? You look like you left us for a moment there, friend." She continued to joke with him.

All Damond could do was shake his head. He needed some more of that, and soon.

"Uuh, yeah, I'm good, Ms. Lady. I just remembered something I need to do," he said as he walked up the aisle and around the corner. He searched the hall for Niko, and just then, the women's restroom door opened, and his stomach fluttered . . . until he saw a flash of red. Angie held the door with her foot as she threw the paper towel into the trash can. Damond smacked his lips and cursed under his breath. She was the last person he wanted to run into.

"What's good, D?" Angie asked as she walked to the water fountain. "You know you never responded to my meeting request with you for next Tuesday. I need to talk to you about a few things."

Damond asked, almost rolling his eyes, "Is it something your team leader can handle?"

Angie noticed the attitude in his tone, wondering why Damond had recently become so short with her. "Did I do something wrong? You've been a little standoffish lately, and I'm just trying to figure shit out. What is it, Damond?"

Damond didn't want to seem blatantly rude, so he gave Angie an appointment time and reminded her just how valuable his time was. "Angie, be on time because I don't have time to waste. If you're late, you will have no choice but to address it with your team lead."

Angie nodded in agreement. "Yeah, well, this I don't think can be addressed by my team lead," she said with a sneaky little grin.

The restroom door opened again, and Niko stepped out. She walked by Damond and Angie without a glance. Damond turned to follow her, leaving Angie talking to herself.

"Hey, hey," Damond said, catching up to Niko. "So, how has your first day been so far?" he asked.

Niko continued walking while responding, "It's been great. Everyone is so nice. Thanks for asking." Niko continued walking back to Tiffany's desk.

Damond stopped at the top of the row and stared at her as she sat beside Tiffany. This chick ignored him and acted like she didn't recognize him. Damond couldn't help but wonder, *How could she not remember me?*

# Chapter 7

Niko and Brielle had gotten lucky and were assigned cubicles beside each other. It had been nearly a month since both women had been on the floor. Brielle was adjusting to the call volume much better than Niko, who seemed to keep getting interrupted by someone who wanted to share call center gossip with her. She then attempted to share it with Brielle, who acted less than interested in the catty talk. She had always been the shy, quiet girl who tried her best to keep her head down and do what was expected of her. Niko could talk to anyone, and people were drawn to her.

Brielle would try to mimic Niko at home, not making fun of her but trying to practice being confident and sexy. Her husband, Mark, would either be at work or be leaving for work, which gave her the time to be alone with her thoughts. Madison, their daughter, would be sleeping in her crib, and the house would be nice and quiet. Like a schoolgirl, she would pretend she was single and have conversations with her many suitors. At times, she would sneak the only vibrator she ever owned into the bathroom and pretend that her tall, well-hung lover had bent her over the sink. The vibrator had been a gag gift from one of her friends in college. It took her years to open it and another year for her to buy batteries for it.

She remembered the first time she used it and blushed. She realized that day when her body responded to the vibrations of the small blue dolphin that it was the actual first real orgasm she had experienced. She was glad she was standing in the shower when the gush of cream ran down her leg. She was careful not to use it too often, and she definitely made sure that shc hid it in the one place she knew Mark would never look: inside her tampon box. Brielle knew that Mark would immediately throw it in the trash and demand that she pray and beg God for forgiveness for being such a filthy woman. He would never approve of masturbation and definitely wouldn't go for the use of any sex toy. Mark believed that he was all Brielle needed, and besides, having sex with a plastic toy was a sin in his eyes.

The past few weeks of being around Niko had caused her to use the little dolphin more frequently. Her fantasies were now not only of her handsome lover but also at times of Niko and all the stories Niko had shared of sexcapades over the weekends.

Brielle was in the middle of summarizing her call when Niko tapped her on her shoulder. Brielle continued with her spiel and wished Niko would put more pride into her work. Niko did not seem to have listened in training when they were advised that each time the phone chimed in their ear, it was their paycheck jingling.

Brielle turned to Niko. Her call bar was down, and she could tell a customer was on Niko's line. "What are you doing? Do you need help?" Brielle asked as she continued to notate her account.

"No, girl, I need a break. This lady is getting on my nerves. I have processed her payment, and she is still talking about nothing." Niko had muted her call to explain the issue to Brielle.

"Well, you need to get her off the phone. I saw your average handle time, and it needs to be a little lower, which it would be if you would stop putting people on hold for no reason." Brielle couldn't help but try to redirect Niko's focus because she was interrupting hers.

Niko rolled her eyes. Brielle acted like this damn job was saving lives or something. Niko was not ranking at the top of the stats for Tiffany's team, but she was far from the bottom. She was meeting the minimal expectations, which was good enough for her.

Niko looked over at the clock. "It's time for lunch, thank the Lord!" Niko hit the unmute button and returned to her customer, completing the call. Her screen blacked out, and she grabbed her purse. "Come on, B, I'm starving."

"Ms. Garcia," Tiffany said in her cheerful tone, "let's remember that our lunch break is only one hour, and it starts as soon as your system blacks out."

"Yes, Tiffany, I have been back on time all week." Niko was not up for the reminders today, but she tried to act interested, as if she had been playing by the rules.

"You have, and let's keep improving." Tiffany looked down at her wrist and gently tapped on her watch.

Niko smiled. She really had grown fond of Tiffany. The girl crush she had on her in the beginning had turned into admiration. She didn't want to disappoint her and made sure she did not make her or the team's ranking fall. She now understood what productivity was and how it affected Tiffany's ranking. Her being late from lunch and breaks were causing issues with Tiffany's performance reporting. Now, Niko made sure that she did not go over her lunches or her breaks.

She waved to Brielle, who was still pecking away at the keyboard, and headed toward the elevator. Eating in the cafeteria wasn't as bad as Niko thought once she started eating on-site to ensure she returned from lunch on time. She stood by the elevator, waiting for it to arrive. The door opened, and the Executive Vice President smiled at her. Niko smiled weakly at him but continued reading posts on her social media. She had removed herself from the clubs and most of her ex-coworkers, but she still followed their activities. Working in corporate may have been safer and more respectable, but it was less entertaining. The employees at Charlotte Power were family oriented or career focused. Their drama seemed to be whispered about rather than broadcast. Working in the club was like being on a reality TV set. You never knew what would pop off from one moment to the next.

The elevator door closed, and Niko continued checking her Instagram page. Shica had posted a picture of her in Germany dancing for a private party of women. She was freaking the shit out of some young chick that was about to get married. Niko laughed as she thought about her ghetto ass trying to speak German. Niko enlarged the pic. If Shica couldn't speak German, something was paying off because she had definitely purchased a bigger ass.

The elevator jerked, and Niko looked up from her phone. "Shit, what happened?" Niko said, holding onto the wall. Damond stood by the elevator panel, looking at her.

"I needed to get your attention since you wanted to keep acting like you don't know me," he said as he leaned against the elevator wall.

"Huh?" Niko said, stepping back.

"So, you really gonna keep acting like you don't know me, *Treasure?*" Damond smiled as Niko cringed when he said that name.

Niko had been moving around the office for weeks, not even showing him the slightest bit of acknowledgment or even acting like she knew him. Even when he called the new hires together to welcome them to CP&L, introducing himself as the EVP of the site, she was still disinterested.

The girl had swag, attitude, and still was sexy as hell. Over the last few weeks, he had tried to get Niko out of his head, but it wasn't working for some reason. He couldn't fully concentrate on his other side pieces in those same weeks. In fact, he had to imagine they were Niko for him to climax. He had even spent the last week fucking the shit out of his wife, Tia, imagining her to be Niko. Tia believed their love was being renewed, and Damond couldn't get enough of her. Truth was, he couldn't stop thinking of the night before his wedding that he shared with Niko and how he had been desperately looking for her ever since. It also wasn't helping that Sean constantly inquired about when he would make his presence known to her. So today, when the elevator doors opened, and she got in without even speaking to him, it was time to pull rank and call her on her bullshit.

Niko's stomach tightened for a moment as she stared at Damond. His face was familiar, but she didn't know from when or where. She wondered if he was one of those crazy dudes from the club that she had to have thrown out.

"Treasure, you are still fine as hell," Damond said, crossing his arms. Staring at his sexual obsession, Damond thought of how he had never been with a woman before or after her that made him want seconds.

He had a strict rule of never going back twice once he had quit fucking with a girl. He figured that if he got in a second round, it would make the women think that he had some type of feelings for them, and being married didn't allow for that type of thinking. No matter who he fucked with, he made it 100 percent clear that he wasn't leaving his wife and family for anyone. So, it was imperative for them to keep their emotions to themselves. That was made known up front. Although a few had tried to get back at him by reporting him to human resources or, worse, by trying to contact his wife, both avenues would lead to a dead end.

Damond was so slick that he made sure to set up every chick he was messing with. He would have them take long lunch breaks or days off to meet up with him. They would assume that because he was the boss, he would look out for them, and he would lead them on to believe just that. But Damond would then tell their managers to still write them up so that he would have a valid reason for firing them when the time came.

The paper trail would also prove to his wife why these women would go to great lengths to lie about him to her. He would always tell her, "Baby, they're just trying to hurt me by hurting you. They know the way I talk and brag about you at work, and they want to see me hurt. They know you and my kids are the only things I care about." She loved him so deeply that it was easy for him to say anything, and she would believe him. And besides, she knew how women were.

Niko had been different in Damond's eyes. She had made it very clear to him that there was no need to stay in contact, and now, here she was on *his* turf. He had to try her again, if nothing else but to see if his memory was correct, or if his mind had played tricks on him the night of his bachelor party. It had been awhile ago, and maybe he was making more of the night than what it really was. Considering he had been drunk, it was very possible.

"Thank you. I kind of remember you a little now. It was a private thing, right?" Niko said, relaxing her grip on the switchblade in her purse yet still seeming unbothered by the thought. However, this was the head of the call center, so she knew she had to be smart about how she played this.

Damond felt a physical sting to his ego because he had thought about this woman for years. Hell, he'd spent the first year of his marriage trying to find her.

"Yeah, yeah," Damond said. He wanted to reach down between those creamy thighs and feel her pussy in his hand, but he knew that the elevator had cameras, and Big D would certainly get his rocks off watching Niko's sexy ass. Besides, he wasn't getting caught up in a freaky Ray Rice incident, minus the violence.

Niko smiled and sauntered toward him. If Damond wanted to feel special, she would make him feel just that. Obviously, she had been on his mind for quite some time. She hadn't done private shows for years, even long before she had stopped dancing. Niko figured she would give him something new to think about.

As she got close to him, Damond felt his heart begin to beat faster as she slid her hips across his groin and pressed the release button on the panel. The elevator jerked and began to move again. Niko stood directly in front of him with her ass pressed up against his dick. She smirked as the number lit up for the first floor. The door opened, and she walked out without looking back at him.

"Niko, where have you been? I been down here, I know, ten minutes now, waiting." Brielle was standing by the elevators, looking aggravated when Niko got off.

"Girl, the elevator got stuck," Niko said, turning to look at Damond, who was still standing at the elevator door. She embraced Brielle's arm and pulled her toward the cafeteria. "Come on. I'm starving and can't be late returning from lunch."

During their lunch break, Niko scrolled through her Facebook feed to see what was happening in the city. She'd worked hard to shed most of her stripper image, but she still used the weekends to have a good time. Like pretty much everyone else in the city around this time of the year, she was excited about the events and parties that would take place during CIAA week. CIAA was the Central Intercollegiate Athletic Association, and the weekend was always filled with fun activities, basketball games, and parties galore.

She looked across the table at Brielle and said, "What are you doing next weekend?"

"Oh, you know me—the same ol'. I'll be at home with the kid on Saturday and going to church on Sunday, of course," Brielle said with boredom in her tone.

"Did you plan on partaking in any of the CIAA festivities?" Niko said properly, trying to disguise her intention of ratchetness that she was building up for an invitation to Brielle.

"Ummmm . . . Well, I guess I could take baby girl to the convention center to see what they have going on out there. I know our church is having some revival that week into the weekend, so the hubby will be tied up with that." Brielle didn't want to seem disinterested because she was highly curious about the events and all the parties during CIAA week and always wondered what it would be like to go. She just didn't want to give it away again that Mark would never approve of her participating in the tomfooleries during that week.

Niko couldn't help but laugh. Sure, the convention center had a complete list of family-friendly activities that Brielle and her daughter would surely enjoy, but she had something completely different in mind. "Remember how I said I would let you drag me to church if you came out with me?"

Brielle laughed hard. "Dang, I didn't know I would be dragging you, Niko." She had been working on Niko hard and hoped to get her out one Sunday to hear their new pastor.

"Well, I figured I would go to church with you this Sunday, and we do CIAA next weekend together." Niko had accepted the offer to attend church with Brielle, and now, her offer was on the table for Brielle to accept.

Brielle's face contorted into a confused frown. "Ooooh, I don't know, Niko. I've heard it gets kinda crazy during CIAA. Can't we just go out to eat when the city's not so crowded?"

"No, ma'am. A deal is a deal. Besides, going out to eat is *not* the same as *going out*. C'mon, Bri. I don't know how often or even if this opportunity will reoccur. So, go ahead and get your sitter on deck because we're going out next weekend," Niko said with a wide grin.

"OK, but that means church *this* Sunday," Brielle responded with a partial smile to match Niko's wide grin. Brielle hoped that after Niko heard her pastor preach, she wouldn't think about CIAA at all.

# Chapter 8

Sean hummed along to the Young Jeezy song on his office radio. He was working on a new reporting program. His office was at the far end of the call center, which he loved. People had to walk by his office to get to the elevators, which gave him, in most cases, lovely views of the women in the office. He didn't even hear the knock at his door as he began writing the program code. Damond smacked the desk, shocking Sean to the point that he drew his hand back in a fist.

"Nigga," Sean said, holding his chest, "you know you don't do shit like that to me, man. You could've gotten your ass knocked the fuck out, bruh. Shit."

On any other day, Damond would have laughed and picked at Sean for acting like a little bitch, but at the moment, laughing was the last thing he felt like doing. The feelings that he was experiencing were foreign to Damond. He had hoped seeing her up close would clear his mind of her. It was years ago, and his ass was blasted. Maybe the bitch wasn't as damn good as he imagined and fantasized about her being. But when she slid that ass across his dick and then left him holding it on the elevator, the confidence he had about that night had left his mind blown all over again.

Sean sat down again and continued working on the program. Damond sat silently, staring off into space.

Sean stopped. "Ayo, my nigga . . . dude . . . ayo, Damond," Sean said, throwing a pen at him.

"What's up?" Damond stood, ran his hands over his face, and walked toward Sean's office window.

Sean laughed and clapped his hands at the same time. "Awwww, shit. You said something to old girl, huh?" Sean pushed his chair back and threw his hands in the air as if he were pretending to make it rain on a stripper. "When we getting a show, nigga?" Sean just kept badgering him about the encounter.

Damond shook his head and sat on the windowsill. "Yeah, bruh, I called her out in the elevator just a li'l bit ago. Yo, she didn't even flinch, man, and . . ." Damond stopped. He sure as hell wouldn't tell his boy that she still didn't seem to remember him. "Man, I even stopped the elevator."

"Ahh, shit, for real. Hell yeah. Then what?" Sean was eager to know what Damond's next move was, as if he had just smashed Niko in the elevator.

"Calm down, nigga. Don't be stupid. You know they got cameras in that shit." Damond didn't need any proof of his doggish ways, and if there was going to be proof, he didn't want it to be caught on the workplace elevator cameras.

"Fuck, that is better. Big D could've burned copies of that shit for us, dawg." Sean laughed.

Damond couldn't believe what he was hearing. "Sean, shut the hell up. You can't be that stupid, and I can't take that kind of chance, man. I could lose everything I worked so hard for. I'm not that stupid."

"Hey, man, well, what happened? Shit, dude . . . This girl ain't nothing but another fucking bitch that fucks for money. I told you that three years ago when you went psycho looking for her. Shit, they get paid to fuck well. Check yo' attitude, man." Sean had known Damond for well over ten years, and the dude had lost his fucking mind after a few hours with ole girl. Damn near missed his own wedding trying to find her ass. Sean remembered that even after Damond had returned from his honeymoon, he had insisted they go to the strip club where Moose said she worked. Damond was then, and apparently still was, obsessed with this chick. Sean had to admit that from what he saw, little mama knew how to work a dick. Damond had never let any ass call him back for a second taste once he had it, but ole girl had some shit that had twisted his damn mind.

*Knock, knock.*

"Come in," Sean said, sighing, hoping it wasn't one of the annoying floor supervisors.

"Good afternoon, gentlemen. I'm going to run to Eden's. Do you want something?" Angie said, looking at Damond.

"Nah, we good, Angie," Sean said, returning to his computer.

Angie turned to Damond, who was looking down at the floor in deep thought. "What about you, Damond?" she said, walking closer to him. She had purchased a new pair of skinny jeans after seeing Damond's eyes scan the little skank, Niko, in hers. Angie may have had a few years on the bitch, but she had the body to make her step back and take notice. The jeans hugged her full hips and accentuated her tiny waist and full bosom. The wedge heels she wore were what she felt was appropriate for the office, instead of the hooker and stripper shoes these young girls wore to work. They were a workman's comp case waiting to happen.

She could smell Damond's cologne as she stepped closer to him. Her mouth watered as she looked at his full, soft lips. His hands rested in his pockets, and his white cotton shirt made his dark brown skin glow. She thought back to how he had taken those hands and cupped her ass in her kitchen before sliding his finger into her underwear from behind.

"Angie, thanks, but Sean and I need to discuss some things. We'll probably have something delivered," Damond said, forcing a smile.

"Umm, OK," she said, staring at him. "I still need to lock in my appointment with you to discuss some of my ideas for production improvement. You know, I just received my Six Sigma Green Belt certification."

"Well, good for you, Angie. That's great. Send me an invite, and we can talk. I didn't know you were getting certified. Well, that means we will need to review your compensation, huh?" Damond wanted to seem interested in helping her achieve her career goals, although, at the moment, that was the farthest thing from his mind.

"Oh, well . . . Yeah, I guess so, but I just want to make sure we are doing all we can to be successful," Angie said, smiling. This was the first time he had acknowledged her presence in two months. She knew that he was married and that the rumor mill said he had slept with many of the women in the office. She also knew better than to believe gossip. He was far too much of a class act to slum with the bottom-feeding hoes. That wife of his must have been a piece of work as well for him to seek comfort in her arms the way that he did that night. She understood that the type of man he was, he was staying with her for the child's sake.

"I'll send that calendar reminder when I get back from lunch," she said, touching Damond's arm. She gave him a gentle squeeze and winked before walking toward the door. "Oh . . . and have a good day, Sean," she said before leaving.

Sean threw up a peace sign and continued working. The door clicked, and Sean rolled his eyes at Damond. "Seriously, man, you fucked that one too? Why, though? Ewww."

Damond looked at Sean with embarrassment. "Man, fuck that bitch, and besides, she's old news."

"So is little Ms. Treasure," Sean said, shooting paper into the trash can. "Dude, let it go, or go back for round two to get her out of your damn system. Get your damn card back, my nigga, because right now, you acting like a nigga with his nose wide the fuck open over his first piece of ass. I sure hope yo' ass ain't gonna be moping around like that this CIAA."

"Nah, dude, I'm good. You just make sure your weak ass is ready for the CIAA. You know you getting older, and I don't want to be the one having to carry your old ass home." Damond laughed while patting Sean on the back.

Laughing, Sean said with confidence, "Ain't no way that's gonna happen. Ain't no way."

As Damond walked toward the elevator to head back to his desk, Sean couldn't imagine what made Damond even think of hitting that.

Angie, who was still waiting for the elevator to arrive on the floor, wondered if Damond had said something to Sean about their encounters. They were so long ago, but with what little male interactions Angie had in the past years, she couldn't help but reminisce on the events that had occurred to make her and Damond cross the lines they had.

*"This is stupid. Why am I here on a Saturday again?" Angie slammed the desk drawer closed as she turned to place a file on the adjacent table, and her knee cracked against the open drawer on her right. "Fudge! Ow." The side of her knee tingled, and she placed her head on the desk. "Just great." She surveyed her swelling leg. "Just freaking great, and it's going to bruise."*

*"Miss Tisdale, are you okay?"*

She *froze for a moment. Hearing his voice dulled the pain in her knee. She slowly lifted her head and cleared her throat.*

*"Good morning, Mr. Wilks. I did not realize anyone was here."* He *smiled at her. His teeth were white, and he had a neatly trimmed goatee. She had never seen him in anything except suits with ties. He was always* Ebony Man *or GQ-styled. His suits were not the average K&G specials or department store bought. He had a muscular build but managed to pull off those European-cut suits. She loved it when he wore anything red. It was her favorite color. She often thought that she would love to visit his closet. She imagined everything had its place, and it probably smelled of sandalwood and vanilla. Today, he was much more casual, wearing a white fitted sweater with a turtle neck, loose-fitting jeans, and a fresh pair of Air Jordan 4s.*

*"That looks like a nasty bruise. You need to fill out an incident report."*

*"It's nothing. It will be okay."* She *moved her hand. The skin had begun to darken, but she forced a smile and pulled down her skirt.*

*"It's policy to fill out a report when anything happens on the premises, Miss Tisdale. Let me get you some ice."*

*"I'm fine, really,"* she said, *but he walked off before she could continue her protest. She searched her desktop for the incident form. Great. She was having a meltdown, and her boss had heard her. Yeah, this would be a great way to progress in the company. She had just started at CP&L and wanted to make a good impression on her boss.*

She *sighed as she began filling out the incident report. Great way to spend her weekend, she laughed to herself. What else would she be doing right now? She would just be cleaning her house and watching the women's channel. She was 32, single, and usually bored or, some might even say,* boring.

*"You may want to elevate your leg." He slid the chair over to her. "It will make it easier for you to keep the ice pack on it." She lifted her leg, and something snapped. She winced.*

*"That did not sound good."*

*"My knee pops all the time."*

*"Do you grimace each time it pops?"*

*"I'm fine, really, and thank you so much for the ice. I'm completing the report. I'll submit it before I leave today. I will also have the Calling Times report to you shortly. What time will the Skype meeting be? I don't think I got the calendar reminder."*

*He gently placed the ice pack on her leg. She gripped the arms of her chair as the cold touched the bruise.*

*"Did I hurt you?"*

*She felt her nipples harden as his hand touched the inside of her knee. "No, not at all. It was just cold."*

*He slowly moved his hand. His touch almost felt like a caress, but she had to be imagining that. He was only being kind. She was so pathetic. It had been so long since she had been touched intimately that she was making something out of nothing.* Calm yourself down. Damn! He just put ice on your leg. It doesn't mean he wants to open them.

*"So, when will everyone else arrive?"*

*"They're joining from home." He stood and checked his phone while she felt her temples throb. She had to focus on her breathing. She gripped the ice pack, and he turned his back to her as he checked his messages. "Is the ice helping?"*

*She had to count to five. She had just purchased a house and could not afford to be fired. But he had some fucking nerve, making her the only one who had to come in.*

*"Yes, I think so."* He turned and smiled at her. She bit her lip. Her face became warm. She looked at the monitor and continued filling out the Call Time forms.

*"Something wrong, Miss Tisdale?"*

*"No, sir, nothing is wrong. Just want to make sure I get this sent to you."* He walked closer and stood behind her as she completed the last section. She clicked submit and then maximized the Excel document. He leaned in closer to her monitor. She held her breath—she had just eaten a bag of Doritos for breakfast.

*"You are projecting that we'll have a decrease in the second quarter?"*

*Damn.* Now, she had to speak. She reached into her basket and grabbed a stick of cinnamon gum. She offered the pack to him.

*"Wow, my breath smells bad?"*

*"No, sir, it smells wonderful. I mean, no, it does not smell bad. I just offered . . ."* She felt like a complete idiot.

He laughed and touched her shoulder. *"I'm joking, Miss Tisdale. Lighten up."*

She thanked the gods she had on a padded bra. Her nipples were trying to push their way through to him. *"Sorry, I just ate some Doritos and did not want to offend you with my breath."*

*"I would have never thought you ate things like that."*

*"Like what?"*

*"Chips. You are in such good shape. I just assumed you ate healthy food. I only see vegetables and fruit on your desk."*

*"I occasionally will enjoy a chip."*

He stared at her. She swallowed and then looked at the monitor. *"We have a good average on call times compared to other teams. We have some less-than-professional responses on some of the calls monitored, but nothing that I think requires any terminations. Maybe a couple of coachings. What time is the meeting?"*

"Two, and please join me in my office."

"Sure. Yes, sir."

*He walked out, and she exhaled. She pushed her chair back and attempted to stand. She put weight on her leg and quickly grabbed her desk for support. Did she really hurt her leg badly? Dang, she needed to drink more milk if a little bump like that did damage. She sat back down, placed the ice pack on her knee, opened her Excel file, and began pivoting the data. She sighed and thought about how much more comfortable she would be at home wearing a T-shirt and boy shorts in front of her computer. Her hair would be all over her head, and she would be watching some ID channel. Why was she the only one who had to physically come into the office? This was not the first time this had happened. She could do everything she needed from home. However, he rarely allowed her to do so. She put her earpiece in, allowing the smooth neo-soul to soothe her. The ice had begun to numb her knee when the message pinged on her computer.*

"Can you hear me okay?"

"Yes, I can hear you. I thought you wanted me to come to your office."

"Well, I think your knee hurts a little more than you're letting on, so it will be fine for you to join from there."

"I think I did hurt it more than I thought, but I can make it to your office."

"Just open your Messenger. And can you see me okay?"

"Yes, and I'm sending that report to you now."

*Another ping came on the screen.*

"Good afternoon, everyone."

"Hi, Jackson. How are you?"

"Good, good. Am I early?"

*"Yes, we have about fifteen minutes."*

*"Are you in the office?"*

She bit her lip and smiled. *"Yes, you know sometimes the remote connection can be slow for some reports."*

Jackson looked at the monitor and smiled. She could tell he wanted to say something else but thought better of it.

The meeting lasted for two hours, and she struggled to stay awake. Her input was only about twenty minutes of the meeting. She was so glad when the screen went black. She logged out of her system and grabbed her purse. Then she inhaled and tried to stand.

*"You gotta be kidding me!"* She clutched the chair and sat down quickly. She closed her eyes so tight that tears rolled down her cheeks. The pain in her knee burned, but she had to get the hell out of there. She wanted to get to the comfort of her oversized couch and television.

*"Okay, you can do this. It isn't that far."* She grabbed the door and tried to shift her weight to her left leg. She took one step, holding onto the door. She took another one and grasped the doorknob. *"Okay."* She was breathing heavily, and sweat was on her brow.

The third step caused her knee to buckle, and she fell. She felt arms wrap around her waist and scoop her from the floor. She almost screamed when a familiar scent surrounded her.

*"You are hardheaded. Please, have a seat. I will drive you to the doctor."*

*"Mr. Wilks, I really do not need a doctor. It's not that bad."*

*"Is that why you were facedown on the carpet?"*

She felt her cheeks become hot and looked away.

*"Don't worry. It could happen to the best of us."*

He left the office. She exhaled and slammed her fist on the desk. She could not believe she had fallen and her boss had to scoop her up. This would look great on her review.

"Okay, let's go." He placed his arms under her legs and lifted her.

"Mr. Wilks, I can walk, really. I—" She stopped as he began carrying her out of the office.

"Relax, I'm not going to drop you."

"Mr. Wilks, I can walk. This is embarrassing."

"Well, get over it. I need to make sure you can be at work, and I know you won't go to the doctor. So, I am doing this only for selfish reasons and to ensure the company's interests are covered. You filled out the incident report, and it's policy that a physician must see you."

He pressed the elevator down button, and she chewed her lip. She could smell the faint scent of his aftershave, and for some reason, her eyes were drawn to his Adam's apple. She was such a weirdo—her mouth watered at the thought of her tongue sliding across it, his stubble tickling her tongue.

The elevator dinged, the door opened, and for a brief moment, she allowed her body to relax in his arms. She stiffened again when she felt his hand on her waist. She winced as the sunshine beamed through the door. She thought about those twenty-five pounds she wanted to lose and how he seemed to be carrying her with little to no effort.

"Mr. Wilks, is everything okay?"

"Yes, Big D. She just bumped her knee really badly. I'm taking her to Urgent Care to have it looked at. She's having difficulty putting weight on it, although she won't admit it."

Big D walked ahead of him and stopped at a black Mercedes truck. He opened the passenger door for them, and she winced as her leg bumped the door.

"Shit, sorry. You okay?"

"It's okay. I'm fine."

He pulled the seat belt across her body, his chest pressed against her for a moment. She swallowed. Having him so close to her was causing her thighs to tingle. He finally stood and closed the door.

Big D peered at her through the window, and she forced a smile at him. He reminded her of one of her mother's friends. He was kind of creepy but very protective. Every morning, Big D drove her from the parking garage to the front door in his golf cart. She rolled the window down and took her bags from him.

"I'm fine, Big D, honestly. It is just probably a bad bruise. I'm tough. Remember, I'm a Carolina girl. We play hard."

"More like you have a hard head. Now, you make sure you listen to what the doctor tells you."

"Yes, Uncle Darrel." They both laughed.

"Where's your car parked?"

"The fourth level."

"Good. I'll make sure they check it on their rounds."

"Thanks."

"See you Monday, Big D."

Big D studied Wilks briefly and nodded. Then Wilks started the truck, and Angie tried to sit back and relax.

She jumped as music blasted from the speakers.

"Run to the arms . . ."

He turned down the volume. "Sorry about that. It must have been between songs." His phone rang, and "Tia" flashed on the dash screen. He sighed and hit ignore.

"Mr. Wilks, I know you have better things to do than drive me to the doctor. If you would just take me back, I can get my car. I'm sure I can—"

"Miss Tisdale, you are the only one in the office who calls me Mr. Wilks. Why?"

"Because that is your name, and you are my boss."

"If I were not your boss, what would you call me?"

She studied him for a moment and looked at her hand. "I don't know. Probably just Wilks."

He laughed as he stopped at the red light. "You would just call me by my last name? Were your parents military or something?"

She once again felt heat on her face. This man was intimidating, and he seemed to be enjoying torturing her.

"No, they weren't. It's a habit from college and from being around my cousins. They always called their friends by their last names. I guess I've known some people for over ten years and could not tell you their first names."

The light turned green, and they began to move. Her knee had turned a rainbow of ugly colors: yellow, green, and purple. It also had grown in size, and she winced as she tried to reposition herself.

"You may have fractured something. That looks pretty bad."

"I've had worse hits than this that have done less damage."

"All it takes is for you to hit something the wrong way. The body is fragile and strong at the same time."

"I hate inconveniencing you. I feel stupid."

"Despite what you guys say about me around the office, I am human and have compassion."

"I don't think they say you're not human."

He laughed, and it made her feel warm all over. "I know some people see me as a hard-ass or, as one person put it, a 'narcissistic sadist.'"

Her stomach tightened. Shit. How did he know she'd called him that?

*He laughed again. "Yeah, that one kind of burned a little, but I understood your anger. I did make you miss your flight. Did he understand you having to work?"*
*"Who?"*
*"The gentleman you were going to visit that weekend."*
*"What makes you think I was going to see a guy?"*
*"Miss Tisdale, you talk on speakerphone sometimes."*
*"Oh, yeah. I will be more mindful of that."*
*"So, did he understand?"*
*She stared out the window. Mel had not understood and was beyond pissed at her. When she did finish work, she tried to call him, but he did not answer his phone or respond to her texts. They had been planning that weekend for months, and she had to cancel on him . . . again. He texted her the next day, saying he just wanted to be friends, and she had not heard from him since. He was the closest thing she'd had to a boyfriend in years, but her need to progress in her career again got in the way of romance. The only things she was consistently intimate with were in her nightstand.*
*"I see I have hit a sore spot, and it is not your knee."*
*"Well, some people are progressive, and others have different priorities."*
*"So, he didn't understand."*
*No, you jackass, he didn't, is what she wanted to yell at him, but she just smiled and looked out the window.*
*He pulled into the parking lot and drove to the front door of the medical building, where he put the truck in park and turned off the engine. "Just sit here for a moment. I'll get a wheelchair, unless you prefer me to carry you inside?"*
*"I think a wheelchair will be fine, thank you."*
*He jumped out and ran through the automatic glass doors. She exhaled—what a messed-up weekend. All she*

wanted to do was stay home on her couch with some cookies and cream ice cream and a good book.

She hoped it wasn't too bad. The last time she had crutches was in college, when she broke her ankle falling off the motorcycle she and her friend Beef were riding at the beach.

She touched her knee, and pain shot up her thigh. The door opened, and Mr. Wilks lifted her from the truck before she knew what was happening. A petite blond nurse smiled at her while he placed her in the chair.

"Hey, sweetheart. Whew, you banged that pretty good. Let's get it elevated. Now, this may be a little uncomfortable for a moment, okay?"

Angie braced herself as the nurse lifted her leg onto the metal flap of the chair. "I'm sorry. I know that hurt, but we're going to getcha set, okay?"

"I'm going to park and meet you inside."

Angie nodded at Mr. Wilks, the pain vibrating through her leg.

"Your wife is in good hands." The nurse pushed the chair through the doors and down the hall. Angie started to correct her, but the nurse began chatting about the weather and how she was looking forward to being off the following week. "Okay, I'll need you to fill out some paperwork." She pushed her into the lobby and disappeared behind the large brown door labeled STAFF. She returned quickly with a clipboard. "If you have your insurance card, I can get everything started for you."

"I left my purse in the truck."

"Here you go." Damond was back with her bag. She smiled, took out her wallet, and handed the card to the nurse.

"All right, just sit tight. We'll have you back there in a jiff."

*"How are you feeling?"*

*"Stupid."*

*"Not accustomed to someone else being in control much, are you?"*

She took a deep breath and began filling out the paperwork.

*"Hit another nerve?"*

Was he trying to make her curse him out?

*"Mr. Wilks, do you enjoy hitting my nerves?"*

He laughed again and sat down in the burgundy high-backed chair beside her. *"You know what? I do enjoy hitting your nerves."*

She dropped the pen and swallowed. When she reached for it, he placed it in her hand. He looked into her eyes. She wanted to look away, but they pulled her into him.

*"Thank you."* He released the pen into her hand.

*"Okay, honey, here's your card. Have you completed the form? If not, you can finish in the back."* The nurse unlocked the wheelchair and pushed her toward two large white doors. She hit the red button, and they opened. *"Come on, darling. You can come back here with her."*

He looked at Angie for a moment. She smiled weakly and nodded. She held her bag in her lap.

What the hell had just happened? This was Mr. Wilks, the man who did not seem to have a soul or heart. He was a corporate beast, and here she was, thinking about straddling him and bucking for her life. She had never looked at him as much more than her boss—actually, her boss from hell. Had it been that long since she had been touched by a man—or anyone for that matter—that she was thinking about ruining her career? She was reading too much into his just handing her a fucking pen.

***

"You really jacked that knee up," said the nurse.

"I cannot believe I fractured and dislocated it."

"Well, if you just wait right here, the doctor will bring you your prescriptions. If you tell me the pharmacy you use, I'll call it in for you so your wait won't be so long."

"I use the Walgreens on the corner of Mallard Creek and Harris."

"I know the number by heart. Give me a few minutes, and I'll have that called in for you. The doctor will be back in to check the wrapping and give you some instructions. I'll go get your husband for you."

Angie sighed as she lay back on the table. Damn, she hated crutches, and this was going to require follow-up visits, which she was sure she'd have to try to schedule around the work that "Lucifer" would have her doing. Damn, her knee was throbbing. Why did they try to twist things when they knew it hurt like hell to move them? The door opened, and the tall Indian doctor smiled down at her.

"How are we doing?"

"I feel clumsy and stupid."

"Well, Miss Tisdale, I don't think you are either. It is just an accident. They happen to the best of us, even to someone as pretty as you."

She blushed. What the hell? Were her pheromones on high or something today?

"Sorry, I did not mean to embarrass you."

"Oh no, you're fine, and thank you for trying to make me feel better about being a blonde."

"You are far from being a blonde, and besides, I get to see you a few more times. You're lucky that I am also an orthopedic specialist. I want to see you back in two weeks. Try to stay off of it as much as possible. What type of work do you do?"

"I work for an engineering firm. I'm off my feet most of the time."

"Well, I'm sure your husband will make sure you follow my orders."

"I'm sure he would if I were married, but instead, I'm sure my goldfish will keep me in line."

He smiled at her and handed her papers.

"No husband? I thought the gentleman in the lobby was your husband."

"No, he drove me here. He was there when I hurt myself."

"Ah, I see. Well, here's my card. It has all my contact information on it. Do not hesitate to call me if you need anything."

The door opened, and Wilks walked in with the nurse. "So, will she live, Doctor?"

"Yes, she's tough, but she needs to rest and stay off it. If you give me your email address, I will email the form back to you for Workman's Compensation."

She handed him her card.

"I will see you back here in a couple of weeks for your follow-up." He placed the card in his pocket and winked at her. Then he turned and shook Wilks's hand. "Take care of her." He smiled at her one last time and left the room.

"Looks like you made a new friend." Wilks handed her the crutches, and she slid down the table. "Maybe you should wait to try those. Let's get your meds and get you home." He picked her up and opened the door.

The nurse gasped. "Whoa, now. That is romantic and all, but I have a chair for her right here."

He placed her in the chair.

"Go get your truck, and I'll bring her out for ya."

*As soon as he left, the nurse said, "Well, lady, that is a keeper there, and he's handsome." She smacked her shoulder and laughed.*

*Wilks was more than handsome. He was sexy as hell. He always seemed to move like a panther, and although a hard-ass, most of the females and even some men were in awe of him. Everything he wore seemed to be tailored for him. One day, he had played golf with one of the other higher-ups in the southern heat. She expected him to smell rank and stank after being in the sun all day. Instead, it seemed his scent only drove the females in the office insane.*

*She remembered knocking on his door and walking in to see him changing his shirt. She tried to look away quickly, but she was shocked by the chiseled chest and sculptured abs. She was enamored by the tattoos on his body, specifically the half lion and the other half appearing to be a portrait of himself. She'd dropped the folders, tried to turn around, apologized, and quickly exited the office.*

*Now, she blushed just thinking about how silly she must have looked running away like some geek from a bad '80s movie walking in on the hot guy. Still, the image of him would pop into her mind at times when he had pissed her off. It was the only way she could think of him other than a sadistic bastard. At least he was fine.*

*"All right, sugar, here's your ride."*

*Wilks began to pick her up.*

*"Please, I will have to try to use these things eventually." He stepped back, and she pushed herself up and took a step. She hopped to the truck door and slid onto the seat. "See? Safe and sound."*

"Honey, accept help when it's offered, and make sure you keep that leg elevated. I'm sure this handsome fella will help you with that." She winked at her and closed the door.

Wilks got back into the truck and put it in drive. "You might want to close your mouth." They looked at each other and laughed.

"She's a feisty little old lady. I can't believe she said that."

"Hey, she had a wedding ring on. I'm sure she has fun with her husband."

"I do not want to think about her busting it open for her husband."

"Did you just say, 'busting it open'?"

She covered her face with her hands. "Oh my God, I'm sorry. I forgot myself for a moment. That was terrible." He kept laughing. "Please, stop laughing at me. I am so sorry, Mr. Wilks."

"Sorry for what? We're not at work. I can honestly say I never pictured you using a phrase like that. It shocked me a bit."

"Well, I'm shocked you even knew what I meant."

"Why is that? You really think of me as a tight shirt, huh? I have fun like anyone else. Work is work, but I do have blood in my veins, Angie."

She felt a chill go up her spine when he said her name. She wanted to cross her legs, but that would only cause pain.

"I'm sure you do, Mr.—"

"Stop! Don't call me that. Say my name: Damond."

"Damond?"

"Yes, that's what my parents named me, Damond Wilks. Go ahead. You can laugh. I won't fire you."

"I don't want to laugh. Well, at least not yet. It's a little different. Please tell me, you have to be a junior."

"Actually, I'm a third."

"Yeah, that's what I figured with a name like that." She giggled now.

"Hey, I thought you weren't going to laugh."

She looked at him as he stopped at the red light. His smile made the heat between her legs more unbearable. She cleared her throat and took out her phone. She had to do something to get herself together.

"You should learn to relax more, Angie. Life is too short to be so stressed out." He accelerated. "The Walgreens is on the right side?" She nodded. "I mean, how you responded to the doctor hitting on you."

"What are you talking about?"

"Come on, it was obvious. He could have given you that form. There was no need to email it to you, and why would he email it to you when he needs to email it to HR? So, you're telling me you didn't notice he was flirting with you? You really need to get out more."

"Well, I probably would get out more if I had a boss that would give me time off."

"Whoa. So you do have a sense of humor?"

"I wasn't joking."

"I do work you pretty hard, huh? Well, it's because you told me what your goals were, and I'm just trying to make sure you're on the right track. There are a lot of sacrifices you have to make for success."

He rolled down the window, and the slim Walgreens worker smiled at them. "How can I help you?" she said, smiling at Wilks and licking her lips. Her hair had a blond, kinky twist, which did not complement her light complexion. The fake eyelashes and hard-arched eyebrows made her look animated. Her uniform shirt was intentionally a size too small and hugged her large breasts.

*Angie cleared her throat and smiled at her. "I need to pick up a prescription for Angie Tisdale, please."*

*The girl did not take her eyes off Wilks.*

*"Okay, so you called it in?"*

*Wilks smiled at her, and Angie watched her nipples harden through the material of her shirt. She turned her head to keep from laughing in her face.*

*"Yes, her doctor called them in. I think there were two of them."*

*"A'ight, just give me a second, okay?" She walked away slowly, making sure that her big bubble butt was seen—not like it could be missed.*

*Angie could not hold her laugh any longer. "'Give me a sec?' OMG, what a harlot."*

*"Harlot? Really, harlot?"*

*She lightly punched his arm. "Sorry, did not mean to insult your new boo."*

*"Okay, they're ready. That will be forty-five dollars." The girl had apparently applied another coat of Mac lip gloss. It was the only thing besides Vaseline that looked that greasy.*

*Angie snickered as she took out her wallet, but Damond had already handed his to the clerk.*

*"Okay, Mr. Wilks, I'll be right back," the clerk said.*

*"What are you doing? I have my card," Angie protested.*

*"Don't worry about it."*

*"Mr. . . . I mean, Damond. No, really, I can pay myself."*

*The clerk returned, and it seemed she had also applied some cheap perfume this time. "Here's your card. Whew, I can't wait to get out of here at seven. You enjoy your evening."*

*"Thank you, um, Shayla. You have a good evening too."*

*"Mm-hmm, you too." She smirked at Angie.*

*He placed the bag on the seat and drove off.*

"*Scandalous, and she probably is getting off from here to go work at Candies Cabaret.*" Angie turned red. She sounded like a jealous lover. "*I'm so sorry. I don't know where that came from.*"

"*What?*"

"*I don't talk about women like that.*"

"*Oh, yeah?*"

"*I mean, there is nothing wrong with flirting. If you turn left at the light and then make another left at the second light, my house is like three minutes away.*"

"*You've not eaten anything today besides Doritos. You need to eat something.*"

"*I'll probably just order some hibachi. It's 5420, the number.*"

He slowed down and pulled into the driveway. It was a large ranch house with a well manicured lawn. He shut off the engine and opened the door. She exhaled, grateful she had straightened up the night before. She slid off the seat and steadied herself on the crutches. He stood and watched her hobble around the truck for a while, then grabbed her bags and closed the door. The door of her house seemed to be miles away. She was sweating by the time she made it.

"*Are you okay?*"

She took a deep breath and shook her head. Finally, she opened her purse and got her keys. She attempted to put the keys in the door and, of course, dropped them. "*Fudge!*" She could tell he was trying not to laugh at her, and it pissed her off.

"*Look, let me help you.*" He picked up the keys and opened the door. The alarm beeped. She keyed the code on the pad and hobbled to the kitchen. He followed and placed her things on the counter. She opened the refrigerator and grabbed a bottle of water.

"*Would you like something to drink?*"

"How about you go get off that knee?" Before she could say anything, he had her in his arms again and began walking with her out of the kitchen. "Don't say a word. Just tell me which way to go."

She pointed to the left, and he walked her through the dining room to the den, where he laid her on her large couch and placed a pillow under her knee.

"Okay, where do you keep your menus?"

"It's on the refrigerator."

He left and returned with a bottle of water and her medicine. "Okay, what do you want?"

"I usually order an H12 with a hot tea and extra shrimp sauce."

"All right. Chicken and shrimp hibachi? Sounds good to me too."

"Look, Damond, you don't have to do this. I know you have other things to do this evening, like maybe taking Shayla out."

"You're so funny. Why are you not doing stand-up?"


They ate dinner and talked briefly about work. She began to relax as they watched an episode on ID television. She really wanted a shower, but she was not sure how she would maneuver that tonight.

"Did you take your medicine?"

"No, not yet. They're pretty strong, and I didn't want to be rude and fall asleep on you."

"So, you'd rather sit and be a good hostess in pain?" He handed her the bottle of water and read the prescription bottles. "Well, this one says you need to take it on a full stomach."

"No, you don't say?"

He poured a pill into the cap and handed it to her. Then he began clearing the plates and took them into the kitchen. He returned and picked her up.

*"What are you doing?"*

*"I am making sure you get into bed."*

*"Excuse me?"*

*"Calm down. I'm not trying anything. Where's your bedroom?" He walked down the hall.*

*"Please, don't place me on my bed. I don't lie on it with the clothes I wear in the street."*

*"Okay." He placed her on the chaise. "Where are your pajamas?"*

*She blushed. She usually just slept in panties and a baby tee, if anything at all.*

*"Oh, I understand. Interesting. Well, I will make sure everything is locked up for you." He walked out, and she stood and limped into her bathroom. She brushed her teeth and washed her face. She stared at the shower and thought about how good hot water would feel against her skin, but she could not shower in the one in her bedroom. She could probably take one in one of the guest bathrooms. She could hang her leg out of the tub to steady her on her crutch.*

*She removed her clothes, sat on the toilet, and took the brace off her knee. Her leg felt like it weighed a hundred pounds. She was grateful for the shot that Dr. Rakesh had given her. It seemed to have numbed her knee.*

*She turned the water on and stepped inside the shower. She supported herself against the wall. She was glad she'd had the tankless water heater installed. The water was hot almost immediately. She set the showerhead to pulsate and allowed the hibiscus shower gel to relax her. The pill was beginning to take effect on her. She rinsed, turned off the water, and stood in the shower momentarily.*

*Getting in was easy, but she panicked as she thought about stepping out. She opened the door and wrapped the towel around her. Suddenly, there was a knock.*

*"Angie, you okay?"*

*She cursed to herself. She was afraid she would slip, and there was nothing to brace herself against as she tried to get out.*

*"Angie?"*

*"Yeah, I'm fine."* *She stood there and tried to lean on the shower door, but it was wet.*

*"You don't sound fine. I'm coming in. Are you covered or able to cover yourself?"*

This man must really be questioning my ability to move up in the company after being around me today, *she thought nervously.*

*"I'm coming in."* *He slowly opened the door.* *"Need some help?"* *He lifted her out of the shower and placed her on the toilet.* *"You know, for such a smart woman, that was not your best move. Why didn't you tell me you wanted to shower? I could have—"*

*"Could have what? Helped?"*

*He shook his head and handed her the lotion bottle. "What do you want to sleep in? And you need to put that brace back on your knee."*

*"You're not going to leave until I'm in bed, are you?"*

*"Nope, and maybe I won't leave at all. Maybe I'll camp out on your couch."*

*"What? Look, you're my boss, and I respect this, but this is my home, and—"* *She stopped talking and pointed to the chest of drawers. "My T-shirts are in the second drawer, and the top drawer has my shorts."*

*He left and returned with a black baby tee and boy shorts.*

*"Is this what you're calling a T-shirt?"* *He held it up, and she snatched it from him. He laughed and closed the door.*

*She applied raspberry lotion to her skin and put on the baby tee and boy shorts. She pushed herself up* on the counter and grabbed her short purple silk robe hanging on the door's back. When she opened the door, she found Damond on the lounger watching a boxing match. He sat up as she sat on the bed. Then he went into the bathroom and brought the brace to her. He placed it back on her leg with a physician's accuracy.

"You do know you shouldn't have taken that off so soon."

"I had to have a shower. I never get in bed without taking one." She looked down from his gaze. "Damond, thank you for everything you did for me today. I may not seem like I am, but I am grateful for everything. As you can tell, I am not accustomed to being taken care of by anyone. But now, you really don't have to stay. I'm fine."

She felt his finger on her chin. "How could I leave you hurt like that? And besides, I needed to put my foot up your ass to make sure you took care of yourself."

She felt the heat between her legs again, and the thin material of the robe could not stop her nipples from peeking through the material. He released her face. She cleared her throat and turned the duvet back. She stiffened as she felt him on the bed. He placed a pillow beside her and helped her lift her leg. She felt heat on her cheeks, and he covered her.

"It's late, Damond, and you don't have to sleep on my couch. I have four spare bedrooms. You're welcome to sleep in any of them. There should be towels, washcloths, and soap in the one on the end. Sorry, I don't have any men's clothing here for you."

"I always have clothes and things in the car. Get some rest. I'll be back to check on you." He smiled at her, and she finally exhaled as he closed the door.

What the hell is happening? She slid off the robe and placed it at the foot of her bed. She was hot all over.

*Damn, she'd had a shower, but the moisture between her legs was so intense she needed to take another—and this time, make it ice cold.*

*She heard the alarm beep and looked at the pad: the front door was open. She could overhear Damond on the phone with someone but couldn't fully make out the conversation other than him explaining he would be "back in the morning." She wondered who he was speaking to on the other end.*

*A few minutes later, the alarm beeped again as the door closed. She heard him walking around the other side of the house. She wanted to cross her legs to stop the throbbing that was going on between them. Instead, she grabbed the remote and channel-surfed. She watched a man and woman kiss passionately in some movie on HBO.*

*"Well, that's not helping. Come on, Angie. It's Mr. Wilks. Get yourself together." Her cell phone rang. She looked at the screen and did not recognize the number. She allowed it to go to her voicemail. Her eyes became heavy, the television began to sound so far away, and soon, peaceful darkness surrounded her.*

*Damond turned on the shower water and stepped inside.* Man, you need to get your head together, *he told himself. He let the cold water run down his body for the first few minutes and then slowly increased the temperature as he took slow, deep breaths. He had to get the image of her in the towel out of his head, for he was playing a dangerous game. He should get in his truck and leave—hell, he had driven home before in worse conditions. He had just made it to this new position at CP&L and had already been on Tia's bad side because another one of the employees at the call center had Direct Messaged her on Instagram, coming on some "woman-to-woman" shit. So, he was already trying to behave himself, but he knew Angie would be an easy target.*

*He had already called Tia and laid the base work to him potentially coming home in the morning because Sean was partying at his house, and he didn't want to drink and drive, so he might just crash there. He had used this excuse a bunch of times and knew he had a slick enough tongue to make it believable every time.*

*He thought about taking a shower, then heading back to Angie's room with just his towel around his waist, but he knew that she had taken all those painkillers and was probably knocked out in her bed by this time. He would probably have his best chance of getting at her in the morning when she woke up.*

*He turned off the shower, stepped out, and looked at himself in the mirror. His member was still partially erect, so he closed his eyes and thought about the clerk from Walgreens. That did the trick. He laughed as he thought about her. Angie seemed to be jealous of the pharmacist's assistant, which annoyed him because he knew that this would be a one-and-done deal with this one. The simple idea of her thinking she had the right to exude any jealousy toward him rubbed him the wrong way because that usually led to it somehow making its way to Tia, and he was already trying to get back in her good graces.*

*He folded the towel and placed it on the counter. Then he grabbed his toothbrush and continued his nightly regimen. Finally, he entered one of Angie's other bedrooms and turned on the television. Morning would bring him back to his senses.*

***

*Her mouth felt full of cotton balls. She opened her eyes and waited for them to focus. She looked at the clock on her nightstand: 10:30 a.m. She didn't even remember falling asleep. Last night was foggy for her, but as she tried to get up, the pain in her knee woke her up fully. She looked at her phone. She had a few missed calls and texts.*

Glad you did not answer the phone. That means you are resting. Keep that knee elevated, and keep the brace on it. Sleep well. Dr. Rakesh.

*She stared at the screen for a moment and smiled. She texted him back.* Good morning, Doctor. Thank you for checking on me. I am just getting up and will follow your instructions.

*She grabbed her crutches and made her way slowly to the bathroom. She used the bathroom, brushed her teeth, and washed her face. Then she sat back on the side of her bed to find she had another text.*

Please do not be offended. No, I don't do this for all my patients, but I would like to see you again. How about I bring you lunch?

*She stared at the screen for a moment. She did not know this man, and having him at her house was a definite no. She had dated guys for months who had no idea where she lived.*

I am flattered, Dr. Rakesh, but I don't know about having you over. Can we meet someplace later this week?

I would like that a lot, and I do understand. I guess I will have to wait to see you at your next appointment because I have said you need to stay off that knee. Please call me Nathan.

Nathan, I will see you at my appointment, and maybe we can have lunch.

*A knock at the door startled her. She forgot that she was not the only one in the house. "Come in."*

*"Good morning, Miss Thing. How are you feeling?"*

*"Groggy, but not too bad."*

*He handed her a glass of orange juice.*

*"Thank you. I can't believe I slept so late."*

*"You needed to sleep, and you need to stay in bed. Are you hungry?"*

*"Damond, really, you have done so much, and I know Sundays are when you get things ready for the week. I'm fine."*

*"Well, who's the boss? I know what I have to do, and I have already been working. I have my laptop, just as you do. That will be what you'll be working from for the next week or so."*

*"Really? It only took me fracturing something to be able to work from home?" She placed the orange juice on the nightstand.*

*He sat on the bed and looked into her eyes. She knew she should look away or say something, but she couldn't move or speak. She finally just touched his lips with her finger and traced them. He closed his eyes and kissed the palm of her hand. She knew she should stop, but she continued tracing his face gently. He felt sparks shooting from her fingers, leaving a path of electricity on his skin. He slid the strap of her baby tee off her shoulder and kissed it. He felt her tremble as he tasted her shoulder. He wanted to taste one of those large, delicious nipples. He pulled the shirt over her head and stared at her as she lay back on the cranberry-colored pillows and sheets. She was beautiful.*

*He stood and took off his shirt. She touched his hard stomach. His lips tasted her neck, and his tongue slid over her collarbone. She moaned as his tongue traced her left nipple, teasing it. She caressed his smooth head and moaned as he sucked her into his hot mouth. She whispered his name, and he felt his dick twitch. He kissed her stomach and her right breast. She gasped as he pinched her left nipple and devoured her right one. Her mind told her to stop him before they went too far, but her body held her voice and commonsense captive. His hand moved down her stomach. Her panties were soaked.*

*"Damn, Angie. I have been thinking about this ever since you started at work."*

*He brought his lips to hers and tasted them. Something came over Angie, and she wanted to take over control. She slid her tongue over his slowly. His tongue explored her mouth and made her pussy lips swell. He smiled at her and ripped off her boy shorts. She pushed him back on the bed, kissed each part of his six-pack, and slid her tongue over his Adam's apple. At last, the stubble tickled her tongue and made her nipples stand at attention again. She sucked on his Adam's apple, and he moaned. She kissed his shoulder and placed her mouth on the bend of his arm. She sucked it as she rubbed her clit against his knee.*

*"Damn, baby, what the—" She slid his dick between her breasts as she licked his Adam's apple again. Her mouth was driving him crazy. What the fuck was she doing to his damned arm and Adam's apple? It was making his dick jump each time she went from one to the other. He could feel her pussy's wetness on his knee.*

*She slid down slowly. His dick was above his navel, and he felt her nipples on the inside of his thighs. He felt her tongue go under his balls. She lifted them with her hand and gently sucked the area between his ass and balls. She slowly sucked his left ball in her mouth and caressed it with her tongue. Damn, she was making him a bitch. He wanted to take back control, but her mouth felt too damned good. She skillfully sucked his other ball into her mouth and bathed both of them with her tongue. She slowly pushed them out of her mouth. She had been caressing his dick while bathing his balls. Now, she licked her lips and giggled.*

*"You think you got me, huh? Got me in here sounding like a little bitch . . ."*

*She turned her head sideways and sucked on the vein near the head of his dick. Her mouth devoured the head of his dick and sucked it. She only moved her hand, and her mouth closed tighter around the tip. She moved one of her hands to his balls and caressed them. She slowly slid her mouth down his thick shaft, and as her mouth traveled down, he felt her tongue coming out of her mouth the deeper she pulled him into her throat.*

*She smiled as she thought about one of her girlfriends, who used to be an escort, teaching her how to deep-throat without gagging. The trick wasn't to open your throat but to make sure you got your tongue out of the way. She felt the tip tickle her tonsils, and he felt helpless in her mouth.*

*No one since Treasure had ever deep-throated his entire eleven inches so good before. He could have sworn he felt her tongue on his balls as she deep-throated him. Her throat closed around the tip of his dick, and he exploded down her throat. He did not even realize he was growling as she swallowed. The room was spinning. He could not believe what was happening with her.*

*She smiled at him, and he pulled her on top of him and kissed her forehead. "Ms. Tisdale, I didn't realize you had those kinds of skills. Shit." He had to calm himself down. "How is your knee?"*

*"I'm fine, Damond. Do you need to rest?"*

*He smacked her ass. "Feeling yourself?"*

*She pinched his nipple and reached into her night-stand. She took out her toy and opened her legs. She winced as she placed her knee back on the pillow. He sat up so he could view her phat pussy. She had a tattoo on her left lip of a gardenia. She opened her lips and began rubbing her clit with her toy. His dick twitched as he watched her pussy quiver. He snatched the toy away from her and stopped himself. They both had to be smart. She reached for the blue box on her nightstand and handed him a condom. It was a little late for that, especially since she just drank his cum—she'd lost her head and hoped she would not regret it.*

*He must have read her mind. "I can show you my test results."*

*She laughed. "I have mine on my phone if you want to see them."*

*He kissed her slowly as his fingers played inside her wet pussy.*

*"Wait, what are we doing?" She kissed him again as he thumped her clit. "Please, Damond, I want you inside me."*

*He placed her on her side and lifted her leg. He slid on the condom and played with her ass with the tip of his dick. He slowly slid his dick into her hot pussy, and as he inched inside her, he began pulling her clit. He was careful to keep the weight of her body on his shoulder, not allowing her to place any on her knee. His dick slid slowly in and out of her pussy. He loved the sound of her pulling him inside. His index finger massaged her asshole as his other hand pinched her clit. She felt tears on her cheek. The room was spinning. He teased her ass with the tip of his finger as he slowly lowered her leg to his waist. Then he lifted both of her legs on his shoulders as he began pounding her pussy. Her breasts bounced as he smashed into her pussy. She pulled her nipples and screamed his name.*

"You like that dick? Damn, this pussy is good as fuck. You like it? You been fucking yourself thinking about me fucking this pussy, haven't you? Haven't you, Angie?"

"Yes, yes, every night. God, your dick is in my pussy. Fuck me, Damond, please. It feels so good. Oh, baby, don't stop. I'm going to come for you all day. Oh, it's filling up my pussy. Shit, daddy!"

He found her toy and slid it in her ass, turned it on, and pounded her pussy harder. She screamed, and he felt her pussy explode. Her juices ran down his balls. Damn, he was going to punish this pussy.

She was pulling her nipples. Her voice had become hoarse, and she trembled. Her pussy was making a clicking sound with each stroke. He wanted to fuck her from behind, but he knew her knee could not take it.

"Beg for it, Angie. Beg for this dick."

She screamed as another wet bomb exploded between her legs. "Damond, Damond."

"Don't give my pussy to anyone else. Do you understand?" He had a habit of saying this during the act, but he knew he didn't ever mean it. But he liked the idea of being the best dick that she had ever gotten and that she wouldn't forget him.

She nodded her head.

He pulled her clit hard and made her squirt and scream. "Answer me!"

"Yes, it's your pussy, daddy, only yours."

He exploded inside of her, and his chest felt like it was going to explode too. Even the room seemed to be moving.

She gently placed her leg on the pillow, and he kissed her left ankle. He did not want to take himself out of her. He looked down at her. Her breathing was returning to normal, and she looked into his eyes. He caressed her face and kissed her.

*"Damond, what—"*

*"Angie, we're fine. I'm the boss, and I'll make sure you're covered at work. Don't stress anything. Just concentrate on getting better." He pulled her to him and held her in his arms. They had crossed a line, but it was worth it to him. He knew that Angie wasn't used to this type of dick and attention, and she would be soaking up every second of it.*

*She closed her eyes and lay her head on his chest.*

*"Tomorrow, I need you to make sure that we get the updated call time sheets sent to the higher execs."*

*"Yes, Mr. Wilks." She sat up and grabbed her crutches. "Do you need me to help you?"*

*"I think I can manage, thank you." She kissed him and went into the bathroom.*

*Her text message whistled. He picked up the phone and read the text across the top:* I want to see you before your appointment. Tell me where your office is, and I'll bring you lunch.

*He sat up and placed the phone on the nightstand. He chuckled at the fact that the doctor was bold enough to text her and hoped that she would text him back and take him up on the offer. He knew he wasn't going to try to double back and wanted Angie to have a distraction from him, but he knew the type of pipe he just laid would have her wanting more. He decided to get himself together and leave as soon as possible.*

*Little did he know that he would end up being Angie's "Villain Origin Story" of her being the biggest bitch around the office. All of the anger from Damond getting back to the office and completely brushing her off made her blood boil, and she knew that any new pretty thing that started at the call center would be the new subject of Damond's attention.*

***

    Angie quickly snapped herself out of the trance of reminiscing about him and got into her car. She thought how stupid she was to have believed that she and Damond would be an item and how she wished she had given that doctor the time of day. Maybe she'd have a man right now instead of heading back home to get on her big couch in her big, empty house, curl up with some cookies and cream, and watch her ID channel like every evening.

# Chapter 9

Niko texted Mystic, one of the few chicks from the club she still kept in contact with. Mystic left the club a few months before Niko to work as a paralegal.

"Girl, we got fifteen minutes," Brielle said, sipping her tea. "You have been unusually quiet. Everything okay?"

"I'm good, boo," Niko said as she began to eat her salad.

Brielle studied Niko. She wanted to press her to find out what was really bothering her, but from the little she knew about Niko, she knew she shouldn't push too hard. "I'm excited about you joining us in church Sunday. I know you are going to have a good time," Brielle said, trying to bring some light into Niko's mood.

"Uh . . . Oh, yeah, church," Niko said, rolling her eyes and mockingly raising her hand in praise.

"Girl, worshiping the heavenly Father will make whatever is bothering your spirit disappear. Some good ol' singing and praise is just what you need," Brielle said, waving her hand. "It will wash everything away, honey. The Holy Spirit will give you a feeling like nothing else on this planet. Just trust and believe."

Niko nodded and crunched a carrot.

The rest of the day went by quickly. Niko locked her desk and said goodbye to her teammates. Brielle, as usual, was stuck on a call. Niko tapped her shoulder, waved goodbye, and grabbed her bag. She didn't feel like hanging around, waiting for Brielle. She really wanted to get home and chill for a little bit. Mystic had hit her back, and they would meet for drinks later. As she neared the end of the row, Damond appeared and smiled at her.

"Ms. Garcia, may I see you in my office?" Damond said.

"Well, I am off and need to get home." Niko was looking down in her handbag, scrambling for her keys.

"I just need a moment of your time. Tiffany was supposed to send you to my office earlier. I guess she forgot to send you the email." Damond was not taking no for an answer and, of course, he wanted to make things sound business related.

Niko sighed. Tiffany sent the email saying he wanted to see her and another agent from the team, but she had forgotten until he had just reminded her. Niko left her desk when she said he wanted to see her but went into the break room instead. She didn't want to deal with him being flirty, so she stayed in the bathroom for about fifteen minutes and then returned to her desk. Now that she thought about it, it would have been better for her to go with her teammate. Then she wouldn't have been alone with this dude. The memory of him was still fuzzy for her.

"Am I in trouble?" she asked.

"No, not at all. It's the complete opposite," Damond said, taking her elbow to guide her to the elevators. Niko's glare caused him to release her arm. "Please."

Niko put her bags on her shoulder, looking back at Brielle, hoping she was off the phone. But Brielle just reclined back in her seat, which meant she would be a minute. Niko smiled at Damond and walked with him to the elevator. He pressed the up button.

Niko took out her phone and began checking her Instagram page. She noticed a friend request from Rho and immediately accepted it. She began scanning through Rho's profile. Rho was still fly as hell, and every pic looked as though Rho had been in a professional photo shoot. However, she couldn't stop thinking about how annoyed she was about Damond's interruption from getting her weekend started.

The doors opened, and she followed him to the end of the hall. He opened the large, black door, and she stepped inside. His office was as large as the break room. African art hung on the wall, along with awards and pictures of Damond at different events in the city.

"Have a seat, Treasure," Damond said, smirking.

Niko rolled her eyes. She didn't know what this nigga wanted, but whatever it was, she was going to play her hand right and use it to her advantage. "I don't go by that name anymore," she said, rolling her eyes in disgust.

"So, obviously, you remember me from the club or something," Damond hinted.

Niko put her phone in her purse, crossed her legs, and looked into Damond's eyes. "What is it that you need?" she said with annoyance.

Damond was taken aback by her attitude. She didn't even acknowledge his position or who he was in her life right now.

"You *really* don't remember me . . . do you?" he asked, standing and walking around his large mahogany desk. "Well, should I do something to help jog your memory?"

Damond was not hard on the eyes at all and was the head of the call center. She had dealt with worse, and dealing with this dude might not be bad. Like a typical man, his ego was getting the best of him, and she really did *not* remember him. Although his face was somewhat familiar to her, she couldn't find him in her memory before the call center.

Damond couldn't read Niko's expression, so he cleared his throat and walked to his bar. "Would you like something to drink?" he asked as he poured himself some Cîroc. "It's okay. It's after hours."

Niko stood up and walked over to Damond. She wasn't quite sure about her last encounter with him, but she damn well knew he was the boss, and she definitely wanted to remain in good graces with him. She leaned in close behind Damond. He could feel her breath on his neck; she was just that close. Her hand pulled up his shirt and caressed his stomach. She slid her pointer fingernail down the dip of his six-pack.

He heard Kelly Rowland's "Motivation" playing on the radio behind him. Niko pressed her soft breasts onto his back. Damond attempted to turn around, but Niko held him in place and kissed the back of his neck. He tried to hold back, but a low moan escaped his throat as her hand began to unbutton his jeans. She teased his hairline with her fingers, sliding her tongue behind his left ear.

"Umm, damn," Niko said as her hand found its way to his swollen dick. "Damn, daddy, I don't know how I could forget *this*," she said, stroking his dick with her right hand. She slid her left hand up to his nipple and gently began pulling it between her index and thumb. She smiled as Damond's head fell back onto her shoulder. She knew how to control men, even when they thought they were the kings of their land.

Then Niko placed her long leg on the top of the bar, allowing Damond's hand to reach back in search of her sweet little wet box. He managed to slide his nervous hand inside of her satin panties. The heat pulsing between her legs was driving him crazy.

"Shit," Damond said as his finger found her bulging clit. Niko gasped as he began to work her button. She purred in his ear, gripping his manhood as it continued to stiffen in her hand. She squeezed the base of it, preventing his release.

"No, we can't do this at work," she said, stepping away from him and adjusting her skirt.

Damond's knees almost buckled. He grabbed the bar to steady himself. Niko giggled as she watched Damond attempt to gather himself.

"What you mean no? Don't worry. We can do whatever we want to do . . . I'm the boss, remember? Please, don't leave me like this." Damond did not want Niko to stop. That little bit had confirmed *Treasure* to be precisely who Damond and Sean thought she was.

"No, it wouldn't be right, and I'm more of a lady than that. You gotta work for this. But I *will* leave you with a little something."

She took off her soaked satin panties and placed them on his shoulder.

The scent of her pussy was the same sweetness he remembered from the night of his bachelor party. "Fine, but give me a chance, Niko. Go out with me this weekend," Damond begged, turning around and trying to fix his clothes. Her large eyes pulled at his soul.

"Sorry, I can't. I have plans this weekend," Niko said, checking her hair in the mirror behind his desk.

"Well then, how about next weekend or one day next week? We need to finish this shit," Damond said, grabbing her soft ass and pulling her to him.

"We do? Why, Damond?" Niko looked confused, trying to pull away from him.

Damond couldn't answer her, and for the first time since he ever could stick his dick in a chick, he was at a loss for words. He just couldn't find the words he needed to woo her.

"Look, I really have to go," Niko said, returning to the chair to grab her bag.

"Wait, here," Damond said, walking to his desk and opening the drawer. "You won these."

Niko looked at the tickets. "Wow. VIP passes for the weekend. How did I win these?"

Damond smirked at her, and she shrugged, walking toward the door.

"I want to take you out, Ms. Garcia . . . seriously," Damond said sternly.

"Yeah, I heard ya. Have a good weekend, Mr. Wilks."

The door clicked, and Damond fell into his chair. He stared at the door. This girl had done it to him again, leaving him wanting more of her, and this time, she had done it on his own fucking turf.

# Chapter 10

Brielle darted her head toward the entrance of the church every few minutes, trying to catch Niko's arrival. When she finally came through the church doors, Brielle smiled, happy that she had not been stood up. She had been talking to her husband about Niko for weeks and was excited that they would finally meet. She noticed that Niko's dress was simple enough, a floral printed wrap dress that most of the other women at the church wouldn't dare wear, but it was presentable. The dress itself wasn't too sexy or revealing. It was the way Niko's hips bowed out at her waist and the plumpness of her breasts that made it appear a bit secular.

Niko sashayed into the church, looking for a seat that wasn't too close to the front. She found a seat on a pew near the back of the sanctuary and sat down, ignoring the usher's direction to a seat much closer to the pulpit. As she settled in and began to bob her head to the music, she was startled by a hand on her shoulder. She looked up to see Brielle grinning down at her.

"Come on, girl," she said. "Come sit with me and my family."

Without a word, Niko stood and followed Brielle's instructions.

She wasn't the least bit surprised as she was navigated to a seat that was damn near on top of the pulpit. Over the last few weeks, Niko and Brielle had started to form a genuine bond that neither of them had expected, especially not in such a short period. Niko admired how Brielle balanced her family needs with the stresses of a new job. On the other hand, Brielle looked forward to hearing Niko's escapades of the single life that she'd never been able to experience herself. She didn't regret getting married or having her daughter, but she secretly wished she'd waited longer to settle down.

As the two women scooted into their seats, Niko was immediately happy that she'd come. She could finally put a face with the name that she'd been hearing about over the past several weeks. Brielle's husband was not at all what she'd expected. While Brielle had never physically described him, her description of his personality starkly contrasted with his looks. Brielle had suggested that Mark was somewhat domineering and a bit egotistical. So, Niko envisioned a man whose stature matched those qualities. Instead, Mark was not only short but also thin. Niko could hardly believe that this was the man who had been bossing Brielle around. She couldn't even fathom how he'd booked her in the first place. As far as she could tell, Brielle was out of his league.

Brielle's beautiful baby girl bounced to the melodies of the choir in her father's lap. He looked up as they approached, giving Niko an unimpressed once-over. Once they took their seats, Brielle did her best to introduce the two, failing to project her voice over the choir's rendition of "Melodies from Heaven." Niko and Mark smiled and nodded, pretending to hear and exchanging the expected responses.

Niko sat through the service as studiously as possible. She had even brought her own Bible to follow along with the scriptures. Niko didn't grow up in church, but she'd been enough times to know what to expect and what was expected. Most importantly, she knew how not to draw too much attention to herself to avoid being singled out. So she acted like a regular churchgoer, clapping her hands, agreeing with the pastor when appropriate, and bowing her head in prayer. The last thing she wanted was to awkwardly refuse if someone tried to encourage her to go down for the altar call.

At the end of the service, Niko didn't hang around long. She hugged Brielle, kissed the baby, and told Mark how nice it was to meet him. Brielle pleaded with her to join them for dinner. Niko came up with a quick lie, telling her that she had promised her aunt that she would come over and eat dinner with her before she left town. Brielle told Niko she understood and made her promise that she would join them next time. Niko put on her shades and walked down the church steps, happy to be out of the Lord's House.

# Chapter 11

Niko clicked the right side of the screen to access her paycheck portal. She cursed as she had forgotten her password again. She clicked the link to have her password reset. Then she looked at the clock. Fifteen minutes were left in her shift. She worked overtime every day last week and even went to a few parties earlier this week. Niko knew the first parties were generally weak for CIAA, but tonight was when the city really turned up, and all of the fly niggas and bitches would be out. Tonight would be the night that she and Brielle would go out together.

She turned to look at Brielle, who was busy talking to a customer and oblivious to Niko watching her. Brielle was a beautiful girl with the heart to match her beauty. However, in the beginning, Niko found her Goody Two-Shoes square attitude annoying, but she also found it refreshing that Brielle was somewhat innocent and borderline naïve about life outside her church and husband. Niko smiled as she thought about how Mark had scanned her with disgust. She didn't understand why Brielle gave this dude the time of day. He dressed like a man twice his age and behaved like he lived in the '50s. Brielle had already told Niko that he treated her more like a child than a wife.

Niko had given Brielle a pair of large gold hoop earrings to wear. They looked really cute on her when she wore her hair up. The next day, she came to work with the earrings in the box. She told Niko how much she loved them, but Mark disapproved. Niko would have protested, but she could tell that Brielle had been crying, which pissed her off. She decided not to push the issue but put the earrings in her desk drawer.

Brielle completed her last call, locked up her headset, and began packing to leave. Niko followed suit, standing up and stretching.

"Ladies, enjoy your weekend," Quentin said as he walked by their cubicles.

"You too, Q," Niko said, smiling. Quentin had always behaved like a gentleman. Niko had observed him going to lunch with Damond and Sean, but he didn't seem to be like them. If he knew anything about her past, he never made any sideways comments or treated her differently than the first day she met him.

Brielle grabbed her keys. "All right, lady. I'm going to head home, change, and drop the baby off. Mark has a meeting tonight at the church, and then he has his meeting with a Hundred Black Men after that. What time should I be at your place?"

"Girl, now, you know you don't have to do this," Niko said, praying that Brielle wouldn't renege on her plans to go. "I don't want to cause no issues with your marriage."

"No . . . Mark and I discussed it. It will be fine. I told him I just wanted to go out with friends from work." Brielle tried to make everything seem OK with Niko. She didn't tell him she was going out only with Niko, as Mark had made it clear he disapproved of her, even after Brielle told him that Niko was a good person and that she could bring her to the Lord. Mark told her she could speak to her at work, and that should be the extent of it. He said Niko wasn't anything good, and he wanted Brielle to stay away from her outside of that. He told Brielle that he could look at her and tell she had no morals, which would ultimately drag Brielle down and possibly ruin their marriage if she got too close to her.

Brielle had called her mother the night before to set up babysitting plans, telling her she would go out with a girlfriend. Her mother was delighted that she was getting out. Brielle's mother would always push for her to have some sort of social life outside of church folks and Mark. She felt that Brielle was too young not to have a life outside of her husband. Brielle's mother never pushed the issue because she always wanted Brielle to feel like she supported her life's decisions. When she said she would marry Mark, her mother was against it at first. She told her to live her life and then settle down after she had the chance to experience things. Although her mother never said it, Brielle knew she did not care for Mark. She thought he was too controlling, and she had told her cousin that he was unattractive as well.

Brielle loved her mother, who was the polar opposite of her. Her mother had been a beauty queen, a cheerleader in high school, and now, a successful lawyer with her own firm. Brielle was far too introverted to attempt to live the life her mother had lived. Her mother had attempted to push her into activities to bring her out of her shell, but they all failed miserably. So, her mother just made sure she knew that she loved her, no matter what.

"OK, girl." Niko handed Brielle a piece of paper with her address on it. "Come on, girl. Let's get out of here," Niko said, taking Brielle's arm.

The girls got off the elevator, laughing at a conversation about a customer Brielle had on the phone who was using the restroom and grunting.

"Hey, hey, what's so funny, ladies?" Big D asked as the women walked by.

Brielle and Niko rolled their eyes at each other, ignoring Big D, and continued walking.

"I know y'all heard me," Big D said louder.

Niko tried to continue walking, but Brielle stopped. "Girl, he's just speaking. We shouldn't be rude," Brielle said before looking over her shoulder. "Hello, Darryl, we're just laughing at some customers. Enjoy your weekend."

"So what, y'all can't—" Big D stopped midsentence as the women disappeared out the door without giving him a second thought. He groaned as he sat down in the chair, watching them on the camera, walking arm in arm to their cars. He grabbed the giant bag of Doritos and licked the seasoning off the chip. The extensive ringworm on the back of his leg began to itch. He was unable to reach his calf to scratch it. He stood and rubbed his leg against the edge of the counter. "Damn! Woooo, shit, that feels good . . . Damn!" He knew that he needed to go to the doctor for some more cream, but he hated going to the hospital, and besides, he wasn't in the mood for being scolded about his gout, high cholesterol, diabetes, or possible stroke. Whatever the hell else was wrong, Big D had no interest in finding out about it.

"A'ight, Big D, hold it down now," Quentin said as he walked toward the door, trying to catch up with Niko and Brielle. He was interested in knowing what Niko had going on for CIAA.

Big D paused from scratching his leg. "You know I will, playa. Have a good weekend."

Quentin was that dude. He was so smooth with his shit and very attractive but didn't allow it to go to his head. He was sweet to everyone and could make the ugliest chick feel wanted. Quentin was single and didn't seem pressed about having a girlfriend. However, he was secretly growing fond of Niko.

# Chapter 12

Niko was barely dressed when she heard a knock on the door. She raced to the door in a black lace bra and a G-string. When she looked out of the peephole and saw Brielle's apprehensive face, she rushed to open the door.

"Hey, girl," she said with a bright smile. "Get in here. I'm still getting dressed."

Brielle came in and looked around the condo. It was much nicer than she expected. The small space had been transformed into a woman's haven. It had the kind of female touch Brielle had always envied in other, more fashionable women. There was a bright teal sectional sofa accessorized with pillows printed with polka dots and stripes. Dainty lamps lit the room, and a boldly printed area rug warmed the hardwood floors. Her eyes darted across the room, consuming every girlie item that decorated the place, lastly landing on Niko's plump and round behind as she exited into the bedroom. *Damn.* Brielle couldn't stop the thought as it entered her mind. Seeing another woman's body so close to naked was jarring. She admired the deep crease that ran down the center of her back and the way Niko's skin shimmered.

"Hey, B, come in here," Niko yelled inside her room. "Let me see what you have on, girl."

Brielle quickly looked down at herself, feeling a little insecure about her outfit. She had no "club" clothes because she'd never been to a club. She'd pulled together what seemed like the best thing in her closet that was at least kind of sexy. Brielle had come up with some stretchy black pants, a sleeveless fitted purple top, and her highest pair of black heels, which weren't all that high considering Niko wore stilettos.

Niko began shaking her head as soon as Brielle entered the room. "Why am I not surprised?" she asked.

"What . . . What's wrong?" Brielle asked, looking down again at her outfit. "Girl, you know I don't have club clothes like you. You should be lucky I found this." Brielle laughed, thinking she hadn't done too bad of a job picking out something a little sexy.

"Chile, *everything* is wrong," Niko said, laughing.

Brielle plopped down on the large, king-sized platform bed and folded her arms across her chest. "It's not funny," she said with a pout.

"I'm sorry—I'm sorry," Niko said, trying to stop laughing. "I don't mean to laugh . . . but *really?* You have never been out, have you?"

Brielle rolled her eyes.

"It's OK. I have something you can fit. Just take that off." Niko walked into her closet and pulled out a dress that was so thin Brielle could actually see through it. It matched Niko's skin tone perfectly and looked so short that she knew that it would never cover her butt.

"Are you crazy, girl? I can't wear that!" Brielle's eyes were huge. She knew Mark would kill her if he saw her, or if anyone else from the church witnessed her in that dress.

"This is *not* for you . . ." Niko quickly responded. "This is my dress, but *this* is yours." Niko held up a more modest black dress.

Brielle took the dress, looking around. "Where's the bathroom so I can try this on?"

"It'll fit, and you can just change in here. Chile, you ain't got nothing I don't." Besides, Niko had been dying to glimpse Brielle's curves up close, especially without all those *church* clothes covering up everything.

Niko slipped into her nude dress with ease while Brielle slowly undressed out of her failed attempt at clubwear. Niko walked over to the mirror and started to put on her makeup. As she added mascara, she glanced into the mirror, watching Brielle behind her, getting dressed. Her body wasn't fit and tight, but there wasn't any cellulite or stretch marks either. Niko could tell that Brielle's body would be soft to the touch. She was sexy, but *she* didn't even know it.

"What do you think?" Brielle asked. The black peplum dress was fitted but classy, accentuating her curves in a way that wasn't too revealing.

"Oh, yes! Perfection," Niko said while giving Brielle a once-over. "I think the shoes you have will work, but let me fix up your hair a bit, and you need a little more makeup."

Brielle looked at herself in the large mirror in the corner of the bedroom once Niko was done with her. She looked like a better version of herself. Brielle had no idea that she could look so good. She thought about taking a picture of herself and sending it to her husband but quickly changed her mind. She knew that rather than appreciating the sexiness of his wife, he'd find some way to criticize her.

Niko and Brielle drove toward the center of the city. As they got closer to their destination, Brielle noted how crowded the lines were for the party they were going to. She figured it would take at least an hour to get inside, and that wasn't counting the time it would take to find a good parking space.

To her surprise, Niko pulled the car up to the front of the club, right near the entrance of the building. More to her surprise, Niko was valeting the car. They both got out of the car and skipped the entire line. Heading straight inside toward VIP, Brielle followed behind, trying to keep up with Niko's stride. Niko smiled at the bouncer as he unhooked the velvet ropes for her. She grabbed Brielle's arm and said, "She's with me."

The bouncer nodded and replied, "Anything for you, baby girl. Have fun tonight." He motioned them both through.

Brielle felt like she had entered a whole new world as she entered the club. The music got louder, the room got darker, and all the people around her were dressed to the tee and ready for anything the night had in store for them. It was a fabulous place, something like a movie. Beautiful crystal chandeliers filled the ceilings as specks of light fell from them like glitter. Ornate wallpaper draped the walls, giving the space a kind of sexy, eclectic feel.

Looking over the balcony at all the people down below would give anyone a sense of royalty, and as Brielle stood there for a moment taking it all in, Niko came up and slipped her arm through hers, locking them together.

"Come on, baby girl. We got a table and a bottle of Grey Goose waiting for us downstairs."

Before she could get a word out of her mouth, Brielle was suddenly standing before the most glamorous spiral staircase, laced in velvet and gold, fit for a queen. As they made their way down together, arms locked, Brielle could feel heads turning from the crowd below. Eyes followed them as they approached the crowd, and Brielle could feel the energy becoming denser and denser. At the bottom of the stairs, enthralled by the bodies of people dancing and swaying all around her, Brielle suddenly didn't know what to do.

Niko took her hand. "Don't let go of me . . ." she said, smiling as she led Brielle through the crowd.

Brielle watched Niko as she walked in front of her. She noticed her hair swayed following the motion of her hips, and her dress was so tight you could notice the dimples on her back. She had strong but feminine arms and tight-toned legs. Even in the eight-inch heels, she could walk as if she were gliding, not having to look down once to see where she was stepping.

They reached a plush blue velvet booth, candlelit and facing the dance floor. On it was an ice bucket and a plethora of drink mixers. Brielle's anxiety grew, as she knew there was no avoiding what was to come. Brielle wasn't planning on drinking, but she also knew by now that Niko wasn't going for that.

"This is our table. I already ordered us a bottle of Cîroc, and it should be here any second," Niko said as she sat down. "Tonight, you are going to escape your life. There is no husband, daughter, bills, or chores. It's just me, you, and tonight."

Brielle smiled with a sigh. "I don't know what to say. I didn't wanna drink tonight, but you got me in a position where I can't refuse."

Niko smiled and placed her hand on Brielle's. "You're with me. I got you tonight. Nothing bad is gonna happen to you, I promise."

As she was trying to concentrate on what Niko was saying over the blaring music, Brielle noticed something like fireworks approaching them. It was a cocktail waitress holding a bundle of sparklers up in the air and the bottle of Peach Cîroc Niko had ordered for the table. The waitress set it down in front of them with a few glasses and began pouring them drinks.

"What do you like with your vodka? Pineapple, cranberry, or orange juice?" Niko asked so she could tell the waitress what Brielle wanted mixed with her vodka.

"Ummm, I don't know," replied Brielle. "They all sound good, I guess."

Niko, being witty, told the waitress to pour a little of all three into Brielle's drink and requested the same for hers.

"A toast to a hella good night." Niko held her glass up, and Brielle followed.

"Cheers," she said, laughing as they both took their first sips.

"Daaaamn, this vodka is good!" Brielle exclaimed. "You can't even taste it."

"Ha, what you think, girl? I'm gonna take you out with me and give you cheap-ass liquor? This ain't high school. Besides, it will give you a nice buzz. You won't get all sloppy and black out on this stuff; besides, it's CIAA. That means you either go hard or go home. Finish that drink, and let's dance." Niko swallowed the last quarter of her drink, and Brielle followed.

Niko made two fresh drinks, and they made their way out onto the floor. Niko began to sway her hips back and forth like a cobra rising from its coil. Brielle did the same move, and Niko playfully laughed, grabbing Brielle's hand and spinning her around slowly. Brielle's eyes were glistening now, her smile was wide, and Niko felt accomplished looking at her, both arms in the air, swaying seductively to the music without a care in the world. Brielle had a sensual side to her. Niko could see it, and it was slowly exposing itself.

After a few songs and upon finishing their drinks, Niko led Brielle back to their booth. Sitting down, Niko noticed how Brielle's posture had changed. She went from her shoulders being slouched to holding her chest high with her arms more open and relaxed. Her collarbones seemed more defined in this posture, and that was one of Niko's favorite parts of the female body. She stared at her for a moment, and to cure her urge to touch her, Niko brushed Brielle's hair back behind her ear.

"All right," Brielle said while reaching over Niko to grab the bottle of Cîroc. "I'll make this drink." Smiling at Niko, she began to pour. Brielle leaned closer and set a drink down for Niko. "You know what? . . . I like you, Niko," she said. "You're not like most women I know. You have an air to you that I really appreciate. You're just so carefree and independent, and you remind me that it's good to let loose and enjoy myself a little bit. I need you around. I'm glad I met you."

Niko smiled, as she was glad Brielle was genuinely taking a liking to her and the fact that she thought so highly of her. She heard her song begin to play.

*Shine bright like a diamond.*

"B, get up!" she said. "I gotta dance to this song . . . Aaaah, this my shit."

They made their way back out to the floor, and Brielle was really loose this time. You could tell she had never felt so sexy. She was glistening from the beads of sweat forming all over her body, and her neck looked so good to Niko that she wanted to bite it. Niko leaned in, yet holding herself back from tasting her skin, and she inhaled her aroma. Slowly, she breathed in the scent of cocoa butter from Brielle's neck. She wasn't wearing any perfume, but her natural scent was even better than anything you could bottle, and Niko, from that moment, had to have more. Brielle leaned in and locked hands with Niko, both swaying to the music.

For Brielle, the room was hazy now, as if the crowd had disappeared, and it was only the two of them. The music sounded muffled, but it didn't stop her from moving along to it. Brielle noticed their bodies had moved closer as their skin touched, and all she could hear was her heart pounding through her chest as Niko's voice whispered to her.

"*Kiss me.*"

Niko pressed her body closer, swaying to the music. "Kiss me," she said again.

Brielle leaned in just enough to touch lips lightly. She could feel the warmth of Niko's breath, the softness of her lips, and the smell and taste of her lip gloss. She bit her lip, knowing what was coming next. Niko came in all the way and took Brielle's bottom lip into her mouth. Brielle didn't flinch. She stood there with her eyes closed as Niko grazed her cheek and slowly kissed her again, slipping her tongue into her mouth. She kissed her passionately, caressing her neck and collar, and Brielle started to wrap her arms around her as they both began to feel the curves and lines of each other's bodies. Swaying still to the music as everything came flooding back, Brielle had never felt like this. She didn't care if it was wrong, and she didn't care if anyone was watching or what anyone was thinking. The only thing that mattered was that it was only her, Niko, and tonight.

There was no way that Niko could let Brielle go home after she had been drinking. Mark would flip, *really* limiting contact between her and Brielle. While in the car headed back to the house, Niko told Brielle that she didn't feel safe allowing her to drive back home. Brielle nodded her head, agreeing that she had too much to drink and there was no way she could drive. Although Niko hated that Brielle was somewhat twisted, she knew those drinks had opened her up more.

Brielle looked at Niko, thinking about the kiss she had just shared with her in the club. Brielle knew it wasn't right, but she liked it, and that kiss was enough for her to become more curious about being with a woman. Brielle timidly asked, "Niko, would you look at me differently if I asked you what it's like to be with a woman?"

Niko was more than happy to explain the experience to her, but she kept thinking how much better it would be to share the experience *with* her. It was just a question for now.

Niko smiled. "It's hard to explain, but I enjoy it better than being with a man. As a woman, we know what we like, how to be touched, how to be loved, and what feels good. We understand our own bodies and what's pleasurable to us. Men are just good at guessing . . . So, in most cases, we have to teach them everything when it comes to making us feel good."

Just the thought made Brielle's pussy quiver. Hearing the words *feel good* turned her on without letting Niko know what was happening. Sex with her husband was okay, but she knew that there were certain things that only a woman understood about another woman's body. The idea of having a woman explore those places on her flooded her thoughts. Brielle grabbed Niko's hand, asking, "Can you show me what you mean?"

Niko initially thought this must be the Cîroc talking, but she knew this could be her only chance at suckling on Brielle's hot box. This was the golden opportunity she had been waiting for, and even if Cîroc was involved, Niko knew Brielle was still very coherent. "B, I'm ain't gonna lie. I'm crazy attracted to you. I just don't want this to be a mistake, and I surely don't want this to come between our friendship. You sure?" Niko asked, holding back any clues of excitement.

Brielle leaned over, reaching her hand down the top of Niko's dress, seeking out her nipple. Niko's nipple was already at attention just by the thought of sexing Brielle. She couldn't wait to get Brielle to her house. All she could think about was how soft Brielle's body must be and how she was going to snuggle her head so deep in her pussy.

They arrived at the house, and both walked arm in arm to the door. Brielle was starting to display more eagerness than Niko.

Niko asked Brielle again, "Are you sure, love?"

Brielle wasn't even in the house good before she began undressing herself, exposing her pretty plump breasts that had a slight sag from breastfeeding. Even though they weren't as perky as Niko's, Niko still found them to be very delightful. It seemed as though Niko's heart would jump out of her chest, beating so fast. She couldn't believe what was happening and never was this nervous about being with a woman. She had been patiently waiting for this opportunity with Brielle, although she never expected it to happen in this lifetime, with Brielle being married and all.

Niko pulled Brielle into the room, helping her to remove the rest of her clothes. Niko slid her hand between Brielle's crotch and could feel the heat and moistness permeating through her panties. It was really turning Niko on to know that Brielle was so aroused by another woman's touch. Brielle lay back on the bed as she waited for Niko to strip. Brielle was shocked by how turned on she felt that she began playing in her pussy and was so amazed by the wetness at the thought of being with a woman. Her moans grew. She didn't want to wait any longer. Brielle motioned for Niko to come to her.

Niko leaned in as if she was going to kiss Brielle but was blocked by Brielle's soaked fingers being pushed into her mouth. Niko loved the smell of her wetness and devoured every ounce of juice from Brielle's fingers. Niko slowly took two fingers and inserted them into Brielle's horny pussy. Her pussy was so warm and tight it almost felt like her vaginal walls were creating a suction. If Niko didn't know any better, she would've assumed her to be a virgin because Brielle's pussy was just *that* tight. It was either that, or Mark's dick was little, just like him.

Niko stroked with her hand in and out, listening to the moans of pure pleasure coming from Brielle's mouth.

She pushed her back on the bed, ready to kiss her from head to toe. Niko rotated her mouth to each one of Brielle's nipples, giving them both equal attention. Her nipples were so hard they both were firmly pointing straight in the air. Niko could feel Brielle's pussy walls clamping down on her fingers with each suck on her breasts. Brielle began to rock her hips against Niko's. She was experiencing her first orgasm with a woman, and it was intense. Her entire body quivered as if she were having a seizure. Niko kept her fingers deep inside, rapidly curling them back and forth to caress her G-spot. Brielle had never experienced this, and before she could finish her climax, she already knew she wanted to feel that way again.

Niko pulled her cum-soaked hand from Brielle's pulsating twat and licked the sweetness from it. She couldn't wait to put her mouth on Brielle and flick her tongue over her craving clit. Niko lifted her legs, pushing them as far back as she could to expose all of Brielle's pinkness and the rim of her ass. She placed her soft tongue gently in her ass, slowly licking around the rim of it. Niko knew this was something Brielle had never experienced, let alone imagined. However, she was determined to make her enjoy every moment, hoping she would always want more. Niko was prepared to give her more if she wanted.

Brielle couldn't understand why her body was feeling this way. She just knew that Niko was exploring places on her that she never knew felt good sexually. Each spot that Niko touched was more pleasurable than the spot before. Niko slowly began to slide her tongue upward toward her cream-filled pussy. Every part of Brielle's body was sensitive and squirmed with every lick. She couldn't hold back anymore as she grabbed Niko's face, placing her thick, full lips directly over her peeking clitoris. Niko slurped it into her mouth, and Brielle screamed. She could feel the pressure building again as she was about to explode all over Niko's face. Niko pulled Brielle's plump pussy lips back, exposing Brielle's oversized clitoris. Brielle began to thrust rapidly against Niko's mouth, being sure not to miss a lick from her tongue. The faster she rocked her hips, the closer she was getting to covering Niko's face with her pussy. Brielle felt like she was losing control.

The throbbing of her clit in Niko's mouth was a sure sign that Brielle was ready to come. Niko quickly slid her fingers back into Brielle's pussy, again curling them briskly and repeatedly, intensifying the moment, until Brielle's body jerked backward, sending a cascade of juices into Niko's face.

The following day, Niko woke, reminiscing on the night before while Brielle lay sleeping beside her. She leaned over and kissed her shoulder and wrapped her arms around her. They had made love through the night, and Niko savored every touch, taste, and moan. Niko contemplated how the morning sun would bring some realities to both of them about what they had done, but she didn't want to think about the world outside her bedroom. And she definitely didn't want Brielle to get away without one more taste.

She slid her hand between Brielle's thighs until she found her moist button. She began sliding her thumb up and down while dipping her fingers inside Brielle's pussy. Brielle moaned and turned over. Niko looked at her clean-shaven valley as the sun shone through her windows. She placed the small metal knob on her finger and turned it on.

"Umm, ahh," Brielle moaned as Niko ran the vibrator over her clit and licked her nipples. Brielle pushed Niko's finger deep inside her. "Oh, Niko, uh, ooh, ooh God!"

"Umm, baby, come on. Give me my juice for this morning. Come for me, baby." Niko slid her middle finger deep into Brielle's cavern.

Just then, the word "morning" rang in Brielle's ear like an old-fashioned alarm clock. It was morning time, and she wasn't at home. She had spent the entire night with someone other than her husband. She tried to fight back the erotic feeling Niko now had vibrating throughout her body. It was hard for her to deal with the reality of the situation, but she couldn't fight off the feeling or the words Niko was whispering in her ear.

"Baby, I love the way your clit feels against my lips. Let me taste you." Niko repositioned herself with her face under Brielle's pussy. She wanted Brielle to ride her face while her tongue was deep inside until her growing love button bounced up against her lips. "That's it, baby, yeah. You like that, don't you? Brielle, I could fuck you all day and night," Niko said in between licks.

The words coming from Niko's mouth were taking Brielle over the edge. Mark had never talked to her while having sex, and he never expressed to her how good she felt or even tasted. Mark didn't like oral sex. He only did it on special occasions, like Brielle's birthday or Mother's Day, as if it were a special treat to Brielle. He wasn't all that great at it anyway, so Brielle never felt like she was missing out. But the way Niko had just sucked her pussy confirmed that Mark was just inexperienced in oral pleasures. Brielle screamed as she creamed all over Niko's face, fingers, and tongue.

"Umm, soooo good . . . yeaaaah. Damn, you taste so good," Niko said as she licked every droplet of cum from Brielle's pussy lips.

Niko smiled as she enjoyed the taste. Brielle had become hers, and she had no intention of letting her go.

# Chapter 13

Riding home, Brielle looked at the clock on the dash of her car. As great as she felt, her stomach was in knots thinking of what awaited her when she got home. Mark would likely be sitting in the family room, fuming and filled with hateful words to spew at her. The weird thing was that she didn't feel any guilt about what happened between her and Niko. Instead, she felt alive and energized, and for once, she felt beautiful. Still, she knew she would have to face her husband's wrath. Brielle had hoped the conference had gone on late, and he had spent the night at William's house.

She didn't enter through the garage. If he was there, she hoped she could sneak into the baby's room and pretend that she had slept there to avoid waking him. She parked in the driveway of their home and took off her shoes. She cursed as she realized she had worn the dress Niko had let her borrow. She checked her hair in the mirror, making sure it was presentable. Niko had her about to pull it out with the tongue action she was presented on her clit earlier.

Brielle reached the front door and attempted to open the glass storm door. She was shocked to find that it was locked. It only meant that Mark had already gotten up and was most likely on the other side of the door waiting for her. She bit the bullet and pressed the doorbell, awaiting the verbal assault that was about to happen.

There was nearly complete silence and no movement through the house for about two more minutes while she waited for the door to be unlocked. She had left the key to the storm door on the kitchen table. She cursed herself for ringing the doorbell because she could have just gone through the garage. Her nerves were so frazzled, and she couldn't think straight. Just as she turned and was about to walk around to the back of the house, the door lock clicked, and the door opened. She cautiously stepped inside, being met by Mark's glare.

"Before you come in here, you need to go get my daughter from your mother. I called to get her myself, but your mother said she wanted to spend time with her. I want her back here in this house. I don't want my child being influenced by your mother and her loose ways," Mark said as he walked toward the kitchen.

Brielle wasn't sure what Mark meant by *"her loose ways,"* but now was not the time to argue with him. Brielle nodded and began to walk upstairs.

"And what in the name of God do you have on?" he yelled, scanning Brielle in disgust. "You look like a whore. I guess it fits because no decent, married woman would stay out all night and not call her husband."

Brielle turned to walk back downstairs toward Mark. "I'm sorry I didn't call." She stuttered, "I . . . I . . . I had a little too much to drink, and Niko made me sleep on the couch."

"So you dress like a slut, and you drinking too? This is why a woman's place is in the house, not out there in the world around all these negative and ungodly influences. I knew *letting* you get this job was a bad idea. I knew the devil was going to get ahold of you."

"Mark, the devil isn't getting anyone, and I just fell asleep. I love my job. I can minister to those who really need to hear the Lord's word." Brielle tried to be sincere in her words, but Mark wasn't going for it.

"Well, it doesn't look like the Lord's word is being delivered effectively enough. You ended up drunk on that Nevo, Neetko, Niko, whatever her name, her couch! I told you I didn't like that girl from the beginning. You are a married woman, and you need to have married friends. I knew that girl and that job of yours was going to be trouble from the start. Call centers are like being in high school, and it's obvious you're still as impressionable as a damn child. Instead of getting them on the right path, you are letting them get you off the path altogether." Mark was so upset he was barely taking breaths in between words.

Brielle stood leaning against the wall, listening as Mark chastised her for her behavior. Instead of behaving like a husband, he made Brielle feel like a child being fussed at by her parents for breaking curfew. Mark went on for what seemed like an hour before finally suggesting that she take a shower and try washing off some of that sin. He told her to call her mother and advise her that he would be coming over to pick up their daughter. Brielle didn't put up a fight. She knew she was the one in the wrong, and staying out was only a part of the sinful night she had experienced.

Damond opened his eyes and looked over at Tia, who was still asleep, and sighed. He lay there staring at the ceiling momentarily and then got up. Slipping his feet into his CK slippers, he walked into the bathroom. Damond began brushing his teeth. He locked the door because he didn't want Tia or the kids to barge in on him like they usually did. He hated being home because he never seemed to have a moment to himself. Over the last few months, he began to feel as if he didn't want his life with Tia and the children. He was reluctant to hang out with his boys because Tia constantly nagged him about spending time with the family. Kiddie movies and pizza night had become monotonous. He wanted a little more spice in his life than the pepperonis on the pizza.

He was relieved when Tia told him she was taking the kids to her parents for a few days. Tia worked from home, which meant she could really work from anywhere. Damond had convinced her to visit with her parents for a few weeks since the kids would be out of school. He had promised her that he would come down on the weekends, which he had no intention of doing.

As he rinsed his mouth, he looked at himself in the mirror. His mind returned to the memory of Niko touching him the other day in his office. He grabbed his phone from his robe pocket and searched for her phone number. The phone trilled, and he swallowed and held his breath.

"Hello," Niko said in a soft voice.

Damond turned off the water and sat on the side of the large Jacuzzi tub. "Oh, hey . . . Good morning." His mind had gone blank for a moment. He was expecting her voicemail to pick up and wasn't prepared to actually speak to her.

"Who is this?" Niko asked. "Look, I don't need a new cell phone provider or whatever you're selling."

"I ain't selling nothing, Treasure," Damond said in a low tone, trying to keep quiet so that he didn't wake Tia. "Hello?"

"Yeah, I'm here. What do you want?"

Damond could almost feel Niko rolling her eyes through the phone.

She turned to look at the other side of the bed where Brielle had been just a couple of hours ago, wishing she was still there.

"I see you're not a morning person," he said.

Niko was annoyed and wished she hadn't answered. She contemplated hanging up, but she knew hanging up on her boss would be extremely rude. "I am when I am awakened by the right person, saying the right things. So, again . . . What do you want? I know you didn't call me for small talk."

Damond wasn't sure what he should say. He wasn't accustomed to being on this side of the rope. "You know what I want . . . I told you . . . I want to take you out."

Niko laughed. "You don't want to take me out. You want to fuck me. Just be straight up about it, dude." Niko knew how to handle men like Damond, who were used to getting everything they wanted easily.

"I do want to take you out, Treasure, and I . . ." Damond paused. Talking to a woman this way was foreign to him; what he felt himself about to say to her next would be a sincere statement. He wanted to take her out and really get to know her.

Niko knew he was full of shit, and there was no way she was going to fall for his bullshit. "Well, Damond, I'm enjoying my weekend, and it's pretty booked. I'll get back to you about the offer."

His phone screen went black, and then the wallpaper flashed with a picture of Tia and the kids.

"Babe, you all right?" Tia said from outside the door as she jiggled the doorknob. "Damond?"

"What . . . What is it?" he yelled back to her through the door.

"Ummm, baby, why is the door locked?" she asked.

"Damn," Damond whispered under his breath. This was *exactly* what he was talking about. He could never get any privacy. It was either Tia or the kids invading his personal space. "I'll be out in a few." Damond glared at the door. He needed them to get on the road as quickly as possible. The sooner they were gone, the sooner he could get back to what he wanted. Niko.

# Chapter 14

Brielle sat quietly, staring out the window of the break room. Her shift was over, but she had decided to stay and work overtime. Work at the moment was more comfortable than home was for her. Mark had been colder than ever, and he would barely speak to her, and when he did, it was something insulting. He had asked that she sleep in the guest bedroom until she could go before the church to ask for forgiveness this coming Sunday.

Her daze was abruptly interrupted.

"Hey, lady, missed you at lunch today," Niko said as she sat beside Brielle. Brielle turned and smiled at her. People were leaving for the day, the break room was empty, and the only sounds in the empty room were coming from the vending machines.

"Yeah, I had a lot on my mind," Brielle said, smiling at Niko. The truth was that she had tried not to look at Niko today. Smelling her scent and being near her made Brielle want to feel Niko's breasts pressed against hers, to feel her sweet mouth covering her yearning nipples again. She could just tell this sin was going to be one that would require constant prayer for Brielle. She had to keep her lust under control. She knew what she was feeling was sinful.

Niko placed her hand on Brielle's knee. "Well, you know I'm here for you. I wanted to call you, but I know that Mark was probably upset about you being out all night. I thought about you all weekend," Niko said as she kissed Brielle's neck.

"Niko, we can't do this anymore." Brielle pulled away, getting up and walking to the large brown sofa. Niko followed her. Her body was on fire, and she wanted to feel Brielle and taste her sweet lips. She sat beside Brielle, who laughed and rested her head on Niko's shoulder.

"Why did I let you talk me into working another hour?"

Niko looked up at the clock on the break room wall. She was on the clock, but no work was being done.

"I didn't talk you into anything. You said you needed the extra money."

Brielle sighed. She didn't need the money. The truth was, she didn't need the job at all. Mark's law firm made more than enough money. She had initially applied for the work-from-home positions, but after training, she decided she really enjoyed her direct interaction with people in the workplace. She told Mark that she had to work from the office for the first ninety days, which was a lie and something she had never done before, but wanting to be around Niko took over her morals. Now, she had actually crossed the line, and she thought of how hurt she would feel if she found out that Mark was having an affair with another woman, or man, for that matter.

She inhaled Niko's scent, sending shots of electricity through her. Niko gently massaged Brielle's shoulder. Her hand slid down her arm and under the soft cotton material of Brielle's blouse. Her fingers found Brielle's raised, hard nipples. Niko gently squeezed her left nipple, then softly ran her finger around her smooth areola.

"Uhh, umm . . . No, Niko, we can't. Please, stop." Brielle was enjoying it and was more afraid of someone walking in and catching them. She really *didn't* want her to stop.

"Is that what you want, baby?" Niko said as she licked behind Brielle's ear. Brielle let out a moan as Niko sucked on her bottom lip. Brielle stared at her wide-eyed, and Niko kissed her again. She slid her tongue into Brielle's mouth and pulled her close to her. Brielle protested for a moment, but Niko held her tight. Brielle began to respond by caressing Niko's tongue with hers. Niko's hand found Brielle's soft breast again, and she gently squeezed it. Tasting her neck, Niko pushed her back against the sofa.

"Mmm, Brielle, *please,* let me feel you."

Brielle was lost with Niko's soft hands on her breast and her warm mouth on her neck. Niko lifted Brielle's shirt and pulled her left breast out. "Damn, baby, I love these beautiful nipples," Niko said as she worked over Brielle's firm nipples with her tongue. Brielle moaned, and Niko's panties became drenched.

"Aaaah, mmmm," Brielle moaned as she caressed the back of Niko's neck. Her hands slid down Niko's neck, leaning to grab her ass. She reached under Niko, caressing her pussy through her jeans. Niko grinded against her finger and sucked Brielle's right breast. She pushed both her breasts together and sucked both nipples into her mouth. Niko was shaking. Tasting Brielle was just like she remembered. Brielle's moans were making her want more.

"No, Niko. No, uuh, please. We have to stop. This isn't right." Brielle gently pushed Niko away, adjusting her breasts and steadying herself on her feet.

"You want this, B. I can feel it," Niko said as she reached to pull Brielle back to her. "C'mon, B, just one more night . . . that's all I'm asking." Niko slid her hand under Brielle's shirt and kneaded her breasts again. Brielle's head fell back. Niko slid her tongue behind her ear, softly whispering, "One night, Brielle, just one more night. Just let me show you how good I can make you feel. Please."

Brielle moaned as Niko's soft hands gently pulled at her nipples. For some reason, she loved the way Niko made her feel. She never envisioned that she would be doing this in a million years, and she surely never considered cheating on her husband, especially with a woman. She wanted to pull away from this girl and go home to her husband, but she couldn't. Niko's soft hands and hot mouth caused a fire to explode between her thighs. Her mind was screaming for her to stop before things went too far.

"Umm, ahh, we can't do this here, Niko," Brielle said, gathering all her energy to pull away from Niko's delicious lips again.

Niko pulled Brielle to her. "Then come to my house," Niko told her. "We can do this at my house."

Brielle closed her eyes, allowing the fire between her legs to control her. It wasn't just her body controlling her, but also her spirit. Niko made her feel beautiful, intelligent, and attractive. She gently pushed Niko back and stood. The room spun for a moment. She steadied herself on the back of one of the chairs and inhaled. She silently said the Lord's Prayer and prayed for the strength for her spirit to be stronger than her body.

"Niko, I just can't do this. I just can't," she said, running out of the break room, leaving Niko breathless on the couch.


Big D threw his keys on the kitchen counter. He walked over to the refrigerator and grabbed the last Heineken. He pushed the dirty clothes off the recliner, removed his uniform, and threw it on the pile beside the couch. Damn, his tooth had been killing him for the past week. He knew he needed to go to the dentist before it got too bad. Big D hadn't been to the dentist in over ten years. He let out a loud fart and laughed to himself. The odor drifted to his nose, and he coughed.

"Whew, damn. Umm, them damn hot dogs is coming back." He fanned the air and took a swig from the beer bottle. "Now, let me see what I got here." Big D took out his phone and searched for the video he had recorded earlier. "Yeeeah, buddy, yes, sir! Look at them titties! Damn. Oweeeee, yes, Lawd. Suck 'em, girl, suck dem big pretty-ass nipples." Big D put his hand inside his boxer shorts and grabbed his fat, short rod. "Yeah, bitch, rub that pussy." Big D shot his load in his shorts with a few short strokes. He was breathing and grunting like he had just run a marathon. "Yeah, I'ma have both of these pretty bitches sucking and fucking Big D. Oh yeah, fo' sho. Yeah, they gonna be riding Big D's big dick," he said , trying to convince himself that he was actually hung. "Yeah, I want both of 'em up in here naked, fighting over who can suck Big D's dick the best. Yeeeah, mmmm, lick it, girl." Big D shifted his flip phone, trying to get a better look.

"Shit, this screen too damn little." Big D sent the video to his email, connecting his computer to his TV's HDMI for a wide-screen view of the ladies. "Ah, yeah, baby girl, you look so good on my seventy-inch screen." Big D watched Niko kissing and licking Brielle's large nipples.

He was glad he had worked the late shift and happened to be making his rounds on their floor when he saw them go into the break room. When he walked by the door and heard moaning, he almost kicked the door in because he wasn't sure if one of them had been hurt or what. He listened for a few more seconds and then cracked the door. When he saw them kissing, he thought his dick was going to explode. He recorded the entire thing without them noticing. Shit, he was working overtime to save for that new car, but now, all he needed to do was sit back, get paid, and get pussy from these two bitches. He had both of them where he wanted them. He was about to come up.

Mark sat on the porch, looking up at the stars. The baby squealed as she rolled her ball up and down the porch, occasionally rolling the ball to him. He would roll it back, blowing her a kiss each time. His life used to have so much order before he let Brielle go to work at that place. He could feel her change the first week she started training. He was 28 years old and had already accomplished more than most people twice his age. He was successful at the law firm but also had a thriving Christian e-store he had launched and backed his own fashion line.

He'd been working on his clothing line since he was a junior in high school. God had apparently decided it was time for him to receive his blessing. He and Brielle went to the Gospel Explosion in Atlanta, where Jeremiah Briggs spoke. Mark and Brielle had the honor of meeting him and his first lady. Briggs saw the tie and handkerchief that Mark was wearing and inquired about where he had purchased them. Mark informed him that it was his design and felt compelled to make him aware that his entire outfit was his design. Briggs took Mark's card, and within a few weeks, Briggs was wearing one of his sports jackets complemented with a tie on *The National Gospel Vocalist Show*. Fans began to tweet about Briggs's wardrobe and asked about his stylist, and it was on from there.

Brielle had no idea how big of a boost his business had received. He was about to inform her that they could finally afford their dream home on the lake at Lake Norman, and then she asked to go to work. It was the typical thing to happen, Mark thought. *The devil is always trying to make his way into our lives when he sees how much God is blessing us.* He had fought long and hard to get to where he was, and he knew that with God's guidance, he would fight the devil and keep his family.

# Chapter 15

Torry applied the cocoa matte lip gloss and popped his lips. He sipped his cosmopolitan and danced in his seat. Chi-Chi scanned the dance floor and munched on a hot wing.

"Uuugh, Lord, that bartender must be trying to get me twisted, honey. Damn, that some good shit." Torry popped his Asian fan and began fanning himself. "So, pretty girl, you are too quiet. What's the tea, baby?"

Niko laughed. She had been trying to talk to Brielle since the night in the break room, but Brielle had been distant. She would chitchat with her between calls and go to lunch with her. However, lunch had gone from the two of them to the four of them. It was almost like Brielle didn't want to be left alone with her. Two other ladies from their team had been joining them for lunch. They were about five years older and only talked about their church and families—right up Brielle's alley. Usually, Niko's interest would have faded, but something pure about Brielle kept her wanting to be around her. They hadn't had much alone time together, and Niko knew it was intentional on Brielle's part.

Taking the last sip of her drink, Niko didn't want Torry to dig too deep. "Nothing, boo. I got a date tonight, and I'm not looking forward to it."

"What? Then tell the nigga or bitch you ain't feeling it," Torry said as he waved at a tall, muscular guy with blond hair. "Umm, umm, now, see, that is the *third* time he done walked by here."

"It is, right?" Niko said, laughing. "You betta grab that one."

"Honey, if he want it, he betta act like it. Ain't nothing slick to a can of oil . . . Ya feel me, bitch?" He and Chi-Chi high-fived each other.

Niko laughed and slid off the high-back chair. She air kissed Torry and Chi-Chi's cheeks. "Well, I got to go, boos. I'll be seeing yous bright and early Monday morning."

"A'ight, girl, call me when this date thing is over. You look like you going to the damn dentist instead of a date. You wearing that skirt, though. I likes, I likes." Torry looked Niko up and down, giving her outfit approval.

Niko laughed. "Thanks, boo. See y'all Monday."

Her phone buzzed with a text message. It was Damond texting her. He had already texted her three times earlier that day at work, confirming their date for the evening.

On the way out the door, Niko ran into Quentin from work. "Hey, Q, what you doin' here? Let me find out you coming to kick it with Torry and them," Niko said while smirking and giving the side-eye.

"Naaaah, a brotha just 'bout to grab some drinks and a bite to eat real quick. You know me. I keep it low-key. I'm saying, why you leaving, though? You really should consider joining me. I don't bite, you know, unless you need me to." Quentin played it off by laughing. Although he was dead serious in requesting Niko to join him, he didn't want to come off as thirsty to her. She was a beauty, and he definitely didn't want to seem lame and ruin his chances.

Niko looked at her phone. It was buzzing again with another text from Damond. She was getting too annoyed.

She dropped her phone back in her handbag, looked up, and smiled at Quentin. "You buying?"

This was Quentin's chance, and he would not miss out on it. "Of course, I got you, Niko. Quit playing." He exuded excitement and opened the door for them to enter.

Niko and Quentin took a table away from Torry and Chi-Chi because they didn't want to be the purpose of the new gossip around the office. It was easy for friends having dinner to be misconstrued as *they fucking*." Quentin really didn't mind if his coworkers were under that impression, but Niko didn't want Brielle to feel some type of way about it.

The drinks kept coming, and Niko was beginning to loosen up around Quentin. The more they conversed, the more she realized he was a sweet guy with genuine intentions. "You know what, Q? I never realized how sweet of a guy you are. You all right with me, Q," Niko said, gently nudging his arm with her elbow.

"Why, thanks, pretty lady. You're not too bad yourself." Quentin felt this was his opportunity to take their conversation to the next level. "Soooo, Niko . . . Why you ain't got a man? You fine as hell, and I know niggas be on yo' ass. What's the deal, ma? Talk to me."

Niko hesitated for a minute because she didn't want to come out and tell Quentin she preferred to be with women. She didn't want him to pass judgment on her, and she definitely didn't want *this* to be the new office gossip, either. "I don't know, Q. I'm sure it will change when the time is right." Niko winked at him, thinking she could avoid the question if she flirted with him. She never even considered that Quentin was possibly crushing on her until now.

"See, don't tease me, girl. I mean, I do find you attractive and all, but I ain't trying to cross any boundaries that you're not willing to let me cross." Quentin was dead-ass serious about getting to know Niko. He was happy that he had run into her, and things seemed to be flowing smoothly with the evening so far.

Niko's phone buzzed again. Damond was still sending messages, trying to get up with her. She pulled her phone out to respond, hoping he would leave her alone for the evening.

Sorry, Damond, something came up. Maybe we can link up another time. I'll text you tomorrow.

Niko had no intention of texting Damond the next day, but she figured perhaps it would get him off her back, at least for the rest of the evening.

The drinks seemed never to end, and the conversation between Niko and Quentin continued to get deeper. Niko was glad that she had decided to stay and hang with him. She was still concerned and wondering what was going through Brielle's head. She didn't want to lose Brielle but felt she was slipping away. Niko knew the passionate evening and morning they spent together had to be meaningful because even after Brielle had sobered up, she allowed Niko to taste her love again before she left her.

"Look, you trying to stay here, or you wanna go chill at my spot? I got the same liquor at the crib, and guess what? It's free." Quentin petitioned Niko to leave with him.

Niko checked her phone again and turned off the sound, just in case Damond decided to go into stalker mode by sending countless messages and calling all night. "Sure, let's bounce. You got a sista feeling nice with all these drinks we done put down. But I can hang, though." Niko stood up, grabbed her glass, and threw back the last sip of her pineapple Cîroc.

They walked outside, and Niko was undecided whether to follow Quentin or just hop in the car and ride with him. She knew he wouldn't mind bringing her back to her car later. She was feeling a bit tipsy and didn't want to take her chances driving either. "Aye, you mind if I roll with you?" she asked.

"Nah, I'll bring you back . . . I promise," Quentin answered, laughing through his words. He was serious about bringing Niko back but surely didn't mind if she wanted to spend the night with him. Quentin could only imagine what it would feel like to hold her sexy body close to his all night long.

Niko jumped inside the car with Quentin. Her favorite song was playing, "Signs of Love Makin'" by Tyrese.

"Ooooh, this my song." Niko turned up the music and began singing along.

Quentin couldn't help but realize that not only was Niko beautiful, but she could also carry a tune. He let the song play, enjoying Niko's voice while she sang along.

As the song was ending, Niko turned down the music again. "Q . . . I loooove that song. Matter of fact, I love Tyrese's sexy, chocolate ass." She and Quentin both laughed. "You know, you have an amazing smile just like him, and your lips are sexy as hell. I bet you get that a lot. Oh, I know, Q, them hoes be on you, don't they? C'mon, you can tell me. I won't get jealous." Niko seemed like she was pressing the issue, but the truth was, she really didn't care. It was the alcohol that had her rambling at the mouth.

He chuckled. "What are you talking about? Nobody wants li'l ol' me. I'm the single one, remember?" He looked over at her.

"Uh, hellooo, I'm single too, Q. How quickly you forget," Niko immediately reminded him. "Soooo, what if I was to kiss you? Would you let me? I mean, that smile and those lips got me feeling some kind of way. You can say no, but I hope you won't."

Quentin couldn't believe what she had just asked him. Of course, he wanted to feel Niko's lips pressed against his. "I mean . . . Yeah, you can kiss me, but don't feel obligated though because I bought you a few drinks." He laughed, trying to play it off.

They were stopped at a light, which was her chance to follow through with her request. Niko leaned over and kissed Quentin on the cheek. She took her right hand, placing it on his chin, pulling his face closer to hers so that she could kiss his lips. Niko wasn't into guys, but something about Q was sexy to her.

"So, what if I did this?" Niko slowly moved her hand over his groin and began caressing his manhood through his True Religion jeans. Quentin was already rock hard from the kiss Niko had just given him. "Damn, daddy, somebody is happy to see me." Niko smiled, referring to Q's growing dick.

The light turned green, and Quentin was trying very hard to focus on driving, but he couldn't help but realize that Niko was now undoing his pants. He didn't stop her because he wanted to see just how far she would take it. One thing he didn't know about Niko was . . . she was a *freak*.

By the time Quentin had merged onto I-277, Niko had undone his pants entirely and had his joint exposed. Quentin knew there was no way that Niko would give him head while they were driving down the highway, but if she did, he had already decided he wouldn't fight her.

Niko immediately admired the girth of Q's dick. He was nothing shorter than ten inches . . . and *it* was pretty.

"Daaaamn, Q . . . I ain't know you was holding like that. That thang is anaconda status." Niko complimented Q on what he considered to be his prized possession. Quentin never needed to brag about it because he knew *his package* was official. Niko wasn't the least bit intimidated but knew she hadn't been with a man in a while. She thought about how he could fill her pussy, unlike the dildos she had been using to masturbate.

Before Q could respond, Niko had already commenced giving him head. All he could hear was the gurgling and sucking noises coming from her mouth. Q could hardly focus on the road, Niko's head game was so damn good. He wanted to close his eyes and lean back to enjoy. He let out a soft moan and concentrated on staying between the lines on the road, which was hard enough after all the drinks he had just consumed at the restaurant.

"You like that, don't you?" Niko asked, lifting her head, hoping Q approved of her dick-sucking skills.

"Aaaah, damn, girl, that was pretty nice. You shouldn't tease me like that." That was Q's way of telling Niko he wanted more. "You know I haven't been with anyone in a minute. Not that I haven't had offers, but I just wasn't feeling them like I'm feeling you, Niko."

It sounded like game, but Quentin was actually being very sincere. Funny thing is, Niko felt his sincerity. She had already peeped that Q wasn't like most guys, which was why she had already made up her mind that she was giving him the pussy tonight.

They arrived at Quentin's place, and Niko couldn't help but notice how big his house was. She asked, "All this house, and it's just you?"

Quentin giggled. "Yep, just me. Not that I don't want to share my spot with a nice young lady, but right now, it's just me."

Niko was amazed at how clean his place was. Everything had its place, and it smelled like someone had been
cleaning all day. "This is very nice, Q, and it smells so
good in here."

Q didn't want to come across as eager to get into Niko's
panties, because he genuinely wanted to get to know
more about her, but after what she had started in the
car, he was ready to hammer the pussy. Quentin grabbed
Niko's hand and led her to the kitchen. He showed her
his stash of liquor, and they both made drinks.

"You want to see the rest of the house?" Quentin asked,
hoping she was ready to see the bedroom.

Niko took a sip and nodded, holding out her hand for
Q to take charge.

Niko walked into his all-white-and-red bedroom. His
king-size bed was adorned with six giant pillows and
an oversized red-and-white comforter. Q grabbed the
remote from his nightstand, clicking several buttons, and
the TV appeared out of his bed's footboard. Niko thought
this was the dopest shit she had seen in a minute.

"Oh, that shit is hot, Q . . . I like that," she exclaimed.

Q wasn't really trying to impress her, but he wanted
her to know that he loved the finer things in life, including Niko. He turned to BET uncut, and the "Pussy
Poppin'" video by Ludacris was playing. He started to
turn the channel, but Niko took the remote out of his
hand. This was her kind of music, but he didn't know
that.

Niko climbed on the plush bed, gesturing for Q to join
her. "Let me get more comfy," Niko said, removing her
clothes. "You should too."

Q walked over to his dresser and grabbed a condom
out of the top drawer. Niko's body was bad as hell, and
he wanted to raw dog her, but there was no way he was
having unprotected sex.

Niko lay back on the bed. He could see that her body was damn near perfect. Her caramel complexion was so sexy against the red-and-white bed coverings. Q climbed on the bed and started kissing her neck. Niko took his hand and placed it between her legs. Q was amazed by the sleekness of her shaved pussy. He could feel the slight dampness that sat in the slit of her pussy. As he moved his finger over her clit, her little button responded, pulsating against his finger. Q couldn't hold back any longer. He began kissing Niko from her neck to her plump nipples, then down her belly. He pulled her legs back, ready to make a meal out of her. Niko enjoyed everywhere and every time his lips touched her. She would let out moans of pleasure. Q's long tongue began to stroke up and down the folds of Niko's pussy. She tasted so good to him, and with every lick, he was sure to tell her, "Damn, girl, you taste so sweet."

Q was good at eating the pussy, but Niko enjoyed it more when a woman was doing it. Niko pulled Q's face up from between her legs, begging him to dip his long, thick dick inside her warm vaginal walls. Q did just that. He placed the condom on and rubbed his dick up and down her pussy to saturate his dick for easier penetration. Then he slid his superlong dick inside of her . . . and nearly took her breath away.

"Oh. My. Gawd." Niko gasped out in disbelief from the pleasure she was experiencing. "Daddy, I want you to fuck me deep and hard. Show this pussy you mean business."

He was having the hardest time trying to focus. Niko's pussy wasn't just good, but she was boosting his ego with her sexual innuendos. Q knew he would come fast if he didn't slow his pace.

Niko noticed he slowed his momentum, so she took control. She flipped him over, jumping on top of him, slipping his dick back inside of her. She rocked back and forth, forcefully making sure every inch was deep inside of her.

Q was having the hardest time keeping it together. He could feel himself about to nut. He tried to regain control by flipping Niko back over, but she was in a zone, riding his dick so good he could feel his energy dwindling with every rock from her hips.

"Oh, shit, baby, I'm finna bust. Oh, shit, girl, you 'bout to make me come. Damn, I'm coming, shorty. Yo' pussy is so fuckiiiing gooood," he yelled out as his body jerked to the rhythm of the words erupting from his mouth.

Niko was satisfied. This was confirmation that she was still undefeated when it came to fucking the shit out of a dude. Niko didn't come because she yearned for a woman's touch. Brielle's touch would do her just fine right about now.

She jumped up from the bed, leaving Q there curled in the fetal position. She grabbed her clothes from the floor and excused herself to the bathroom. She was in there for a minute, and Q wondered if she was OK.

"You all right in there?" he called out to her from the bed.

"Yeah, I'm good. You ready to take me back to my car now?" she yelled back to him.

Q hoped he could enjoy her a little more, but Niko was ready to go. "Uuuhh . . . Yeah, sure," he said, looking around, thinking to himself, *Damn, she just gonna fuck me and leave me? Ain't this some shit*. Niko had just treated him like a trick, and he couldn't believe it. He thought the chemistry between them was great.

The bathroom door opened, and Niko walked out, fully clothed. "I'll be downstairs when you're ready." She didn't want to seem rude, but she couldn't stop thinking about Brielle. She just wanted to go home.

On the car ride back, Niko was dead silent. She had completely sobered up, and Q was feeling completely violated. He pulled up next to her car. Niko reached over, giving him a friendly hug. He hugged her back, wondering if everything was OK. He began to question in his mind whether the sex was good. Then he speculated whether she had come, but he dared not ask. It was questionable because most women faked orgasms anyway. He assumed she would probably lie if asked.

Niko thanked him for a fun evening and got out of his car. He watched as she got into her car. She waved, letting him know that she was all right. Niko pulled out of the parking lot, and Q pulled out, going the opposite way.

# Chapter 16

At 7:00 a.m., Niko's phone began buzzing. She grabbed it, hoping Brielle was calling because she wanted to link up. It was just Damond.

"Hey," Niko answered in a dry tone. "Damn, what time is it?"

Damond was shocked Niko bothered to answer so early for him. "Hey, Treasure, you free for breakfast?"

Niko rolled her eyes, thinking to herself, *Maybe if I go eat breakfast with him, he'll leave me the fuck alone after that.* "Ummm, I guess. What time you trying to go eat?"

"Well, I'm ready now, but I know it may take you a few minutes to get ready. Especially since you sound like you're just waking up," Damond replied, excited that it sounded pretty promising that she would meet him.

"Give me an hour," Niko replied. "I'll meet you at Terrace Café." She wasn't feeling Damond, but at least she would start the day with her favorite meal, red velvet waffles and a fried chicken cutlet.

Damond hung up the phone, swinging his fist in the air as if he had just won the US Open. He couldn't wait for some one-on-one time with Niko. Since day one, there was something about this girl that he was having the hardest time trying to shake.

***

It was 8:20 a.m., and Damond was sitting waiting patiently for Niko. He knew she said she would be ready in an hour, but she was now roughly twenty minutes late. He picked up his phone to text her just as Niko walked up.

"Hey," she greeted Damond, thinking about how glad she was, finally getting this meeting out of the way. She was hungry, and all she could think about was eating rather than what he had to say.

"Hey, how you doin', sexy?" Damond replied.

Niko smiled as a way to show she appreciated the compliment.

"You look nice. Like them shoes," Damond said, looking down at Niko's feet. One thing he remembered about her was that her shoe game was always on point.

"Look, let's make this what it is, Damond. You don't have to try to play me like I'm one of your lames you be fucking from work. I mean, what is it you want from me?"

"Damn, you won't give a nigga a break, huh? And despite what you think, I know you aren't like most of them women at work."

Niko looked away, smiling to herself, thinking about what Damond had just said. He was going to be beneficial to her at this company. Like most men, his ego had gotten the best of him. Niko had watched him around the office, smiling and charming the simpleminded females of the center. Working in this place was actually worse than working at the club. At least at the club, people were who they were. They didn't hide behind facades of scriptures or college degrees. The only difference between the women at the call center and the club was about thirty to forty pounds.

Damond began making small talk, and Niko nodded or responded with one-word answers.

"May I borrow your phone for a moment?" Niko asked. "I need to charge mine. This new iPhone has a horrible battery life."

Damond nodded and handed her his phone. "See, that's why I like Galaxy. Samsung is a superior product. Look, I'ma run to the bathroom real quick." Damond stood up and excused himself.

Niko opened a new text message.

Hey, I'm having breakfast with a friend, but I'm thinking of you. I miss you so much, baby. I want to see you soon. I need to see you . . . just the two of us. I can't get the other night out of my mind. I don't want to make your home life any harder than it is. He doesn't love you like I do, and he sure as hell don't deserve you.

Niko hit send and sighed. She stared at the screen. She couldn't believe she typed those words, especially from someone else's phone, but she knew Mark wouldn't be so suspicious if an incoming message came in from Brielle's boss. Niko already knew she was not one of his favorites.

Niko felt better now that she had sent the message. She breathed a sigh of relief again, and for some reason, she felt her stomach relax.

Mark poured the buttermilk into the bowl and checked the tablet for the next ingredient. Brielle's phone vibrated three times. He looked into the family room, where Brielle and Misty played with blocks. The screen lit up, showing that she had text messages. He swiped the screen, but only a number was displayed. He looked back into the family room, then at the phone. He washed his hands and picked up the phone . . . and his heart stopped as he read the text.

Misty squealed as Brielle knocked down the blocks. Mark steadied himself against the counter as he read the words on the screen. He forwarded the text to his cell phone and then deleted it from Brielle's. The room began to move. He blinked his eyes, and every object in front of him doubled.

"Mark? Are you okay?" Brielle asked as she entered the kitchen, placing Misty in the high chair. Mark's throat was dry. He tried not to make eye contact with Brielle out of fear that he would strangle her. *This can't be life right now. She's having an affair,* he thought. The last thing he needed right now was a scandal associated with his name. He had to handle this delicately and intelligently.

His hands shook as he picked up the large butcher knife. He paused over the cutting board as Brielle walked by, going to the refrigerator.

"Mark?" Brielle said as she placed the orange juice on the counter.

"Yeah, yeah, I'm good. Onions, you know, they can get to you sometimes." Mark tried to play it off, wiping his eyes.

Brielle smiled and poured the juice into Misty's cup. "OK, well, I'll give her a bath after she finishes her juice." Mark nodded. Brielle kissed his cheek and placed the juice back inside the refrigerator.

He watched her pick up Misty and walk toward the family room. She was a beautiful woman. Many times, he had heard people say that he was lucky she was such a humble woman. She was out of his league and could have definitely done better than him.

Mark was a short man, and he was well below average in the looks department. At times, when he and Brielle were out, men would blatantly try to hit on her in front of him. He had, of course, handled it with couth, but when he got Brielle alone, he made sure she understood how lucky she was to have him. He reminded her that it was God's plan for her to be with him, and the other men only wanted her body and her soul damned.

Until now, Brielle had been a good girl despite being raised by a harlot of a mother. He was grateful for her grandmother's influence on keeping her head straight and out of the world. He knew allowing her to work at that call center would be a mistake. He was well known around Charlotte and the surrounding areas. The devil was always busy, Mark's blessings were right within his reach, and he had to ensure that nothing or no one would block him from having what he deserved.

# Chapter 17

Niko turned to look at Brielle's empty seat. She checked the time on the phone. It was eleven thirty, and she had not heard from Brielle. Suddenly, the phone beeped in her ear. She sighed and greeted the caller. She kept watching the door, hoping to see Brielle walk down the aisle any minute now. Her cell phone buzzed. She grabbed it, hoping that Brielle had texted her. Her heart sank as she read the message from Damond.

You know there are no cell phones on the floor.

Niko continued talking to her customer. She reviewed the account and found that the customer's meter reading had been entered incorrectly. Although she may not have always performed to the best of her abilities, Niko had always received high CSAT scores on her calls. She was a thorough agent who rarely received feedback regarding making errors. She sometimes would forget or not care about a procedural step, affecting her quality score, but she always passed with at least the minimum required stat.

Her cell phone buzzed again. She paused before looking at the screen. Her instinct told her to ignore it, but what if it was Brielle? She decided not to take the phone out of her purse since she would have a break in a few minutes, and if it were Brielle, she could call her back.

"Ms. Garcia, I hope you are not using your phone on the floor," Angie said as she placed the paper in the fax.

"Ma'am, would you mind holding for a minute?" Niko said to the customer. Angie had been especially annoying today, and she was getting on Niko's last nerve. "Angie, I'm aware of the rules of the floor. If you have something to say to me that is not related to my customer, I would like to ask that you wait for me to finish my call." Niko pressed the mute button and continued assisting the customer.

Angie scoffed and turned to walk away. Suddenly, Niko heard a loud crash and turned to see something sky blue fall to the floor. Everyone stood in time to see Angie tangled in the cord of the fax machine. The buzz of the floor disappeared for a moment. Everyone within eyesight of Angie stared at her. Niko covered her mouth, trying not to laugh at her.

"That thing should be behind the counter. Why is it out here where someone could fall and get hurt just like I did?" Angie yelled.

The heel of her left shoe hung on by a strip of leather. No one offered to help her up, so she struggled to stand. As she got to her knees to push herself up, Niko heard the sound of material tearing. The tight pants were split up the back. Angie jumped up and took off her jacket. Embarrassed, her face burned red, and she hurried down the aisle to the restroom.

The floor erupted in laughter. Niko tried to keep a stern face but couldn't help but join in on the laughter. Then everyone on the team returned to taking calls again.

Tiffany turned and ran down the hall to the women's bathroom. As the door to the restroom closed, Niko looked at Della, who sat to her right, and they both held their sides as they laughed.

"That's what the ratchet bat gets," Della said as she laughed.

Niko could not speak for laughing. She was glad she had completed her call because she could not talk or focus for the next few moments.

"Whew, girl. Karma is a bitch, and she apparently don't like sky blue, but them panties, though, chile!" Della said, sliding out of her chair onto the floor, laughing.

Niko laughed so hard that she could no longer make a sound. Her cell phone pinged. She looked around before checking the screen. Torry had sent her a media file. She put in a break and grabbed her cup. As she walked toward the break room, she downloaded the file.

"Watch Out for the Big Girl" played as a video of Angie falling to the floor popped up. The song stopped, and the remix echoed as Angie's pants ripped repeatedly. The reel played several times and ended with a cat running from a pair of pants. Tears ran down Niko's face. Then Della walked into the room.

"Girl, look." Niko turned her phone toward Della. "I can't . . . I can't," Niko said, handing Della her phone.

Della fell back onto the couch, laughing. Niko heard others in the break room laughing. "How in the hell did he do this so quickly?" Niko asked Della, referring to Torry being so fast at creating the video of Angie falling.

"I don't know, girl," Della said, wiping her eyes, "I am done. That cat was too much! Torry is a fool for that one, but that shit has made my month. I can't think of a nicer person for that to happen to."


Brielle winced as she removed the gauze from her arm. She hated it when the doctor had to take blood. Unlike most people, it took her several hours to stop bleeding. She clicked the alarm to her car, opened the back door, and tossed her tote bag inside. She went to reach for

the driver-side door when someone grabbed her from
behind. She tried to scream, but a nicotine-scented hand
covered her mouth.

"Shh, shh. Ain't nobody gonna hurt you, sexy lady."
The odor of Fritos, sulfur, and some type of spoiled meat
molested Brielle's nostrils. She pulled herself away and
turned quickly to see Big D smiling at her. "Damn, I like
that skirt, boo."

"Have you lost your mind, D?" Brielle shouted, scared.
She was about to speak again when a hot, wet tongue covered her mouth. Brielle tried to scream, but Big D shoved
his thick, rough tongue into her mouth again. Brielle
gagged. She felt like she was licking a smelly coffeepot
filled with cigarettes and old cheese. She tried to knee Big
D, but he blocked her and laughed.

"How was your weekend?" Big D asked, staring at her
while he started to unzip his pants. He was sweating,
which caused his body odor to fill the space they occu-
pied.

"D . . . I swear, you better move out of my way and
keep your damn hands off of me!" Brielle was growing
increasingly nervous because the parking garage was
empty. She knew Big D was big enough to overpower
her, and there probably wouldn't be anyone around for a
while to help her.

"What, you don't like when Big D touch you? You
gonna like it, though. Matter fact, you gonna fucking *love*
it. Know what else I love?" Big D paused as if he were really waiting for a response from Brielle. "You gonna like
this bid dick Big D 'bout to give you. Mmmmm, let me
see them big titties an' that peach lacy thang you got on,"
Big D said as he grabbed Brielle by the wrist. He checked
to make sure that he was shielded from the camera. It
didn't help that Big D knew where every camera was and
how to manipulate the cameras to work in his favor.

He squeezed Brielle's soft breast, and she tried to scream. She dug her nails into his arm. Blood seeped from the scratch, and D slung her to the floor.

"I'm calling the police. You have lost your mind!" Brielle yelled as she tried to take out her phone. In the past, she had ignored Big D's verbal vulgarities, but touching her in this manner had gone too far. As she pressed the nine on her screen, she heard moaning coming from Big D's direction. She turned to see him hold his phone up, and she saw the video of her and Niko, with Niko taking her nipple into her mouth.

"Yeah, you freaky li'l bitch! I would have paid good money to see what happened when y'all got back to the apartment. Shiiiit, I bet she licked your pretty li'l pussy good, huh? I damn sho would have *loved* to see that." Big D pestered her about the video.

Brielle stared at the phone as if she had seen a ghost. Big D laughed, putting his phone back on his belt. "Whoo, I bet y'all was like two sweet-ass angels licking and sucking on each other. Good Gawd!"

Brielle stared at him for a moment. Her limbs were paralyzed, and she felt sourness rise from her stomach into her mouth.

"I don't want to mess up your nice skirt, so how about you pull it up so I can see what you got so good hiding down there?" Big D said as he took a step toward Brielle.

"Stay the hell away from me! Don't touch me." Brielle stood in fear, backing away from him.

"Don't touch you? Girl, you gonna be *begging* me to touch you, and you gonna *love* it. Yeah, I can just see it. I'm gonna be like a fucking rap star with two bad bitches at the same damn time, sucking and fucking me!" D said, rubbing his hands together. "I know you sweet as hell. Can't wait to stick my tongue in your stuff." He took another step toward Brielle, and she pulled her mace out.

"I will mace your fat ass, D. I'm not playing. Stay back," Brielle threatened, and Big D laughed.

"I would not recommend doing that," he said. Brielle steadied herself against the large concrete beam. "Yeah, I know you don't want your husband to see this video, not to mention what it would do to his business with them preachers and shit. You know them Christians frown on carpet munchers."

Brielle's stomach began to gurgle. She turned her head and vomited near the white Mercedes. She hasdfollowed the rules all her life, and the one time she broke them, *this* happened. Her fear changed to guilt as she considered how this would affect Mark and his career. And then Niko. The girl was trying to get away from the sex industry and start a normal life. She had only known her for a few weeks. How could she put her above her husband's reputation that he had worked so hard to maintain?

"How much do you want?" Brielle asked, taking out a tissue and wiping her mouth. She dug in her purse, looking for some mints.

"Oh, no. It ain't gonna be that easy. I'm gonna need you and little Ms. Niko to bring y'all pretty asses over to my house. Yeah, we gonna have us some fun. I like the way she lick yo' big ol' titties," Big D said as he massaged his dick through his too-small work slacks.

Brielle vomited again. This time, she aimed for Big D's shoes.

"Bitch, you done got my only pair of work shoes fucked up!" he yelled.

Brielle smiled, but it was a small victory.

"Shit, it's all right. You and Niko can clean them when you come by tomorrow night."

"What? Big D, be reasonable. Just leave me alone. Please, don't do this," Brielle pleaded.

"Yeah, yeah, the money is good 'n all, but I want some of that sweet, rich ass. I ain't ever been wit' nobody like you and Niko. Y'all walk by Big D snarling y'all noses and shit, thinking y'all better than Big D." He motioned, referring to himself. "Well, guess what? I own y'all asses now. That's right, and you gonna do whatever the fuck I say to do, or *everyone* will know y'all sucking each other's pussies." Big D grinned, hoping for Brielle to agree finally. "Oh, and don't worry. Y'all gonna love just how Big D fuck y'all. Ain't no dick like Big D dick."

Brielle was horrified. She felt her blood run cold. She tried to stand but fell back into the car. She looked at him standing in front of her, and the smell that emanated from him was like rotten meat mixed with her vomit. She had never stepped outside the boundaries by breaking rules, and the first time she did, this was what happened.

"I'll start with you first. Just bring your li'l pretty ass to my house tonight at 9:30. Yeah, I'm gonna have me some fun with dis here, and if you don't show up, not only will I make sure your husband gets a copy of this, but it will also be all over worldstar.com and Facebook." Big D threatened her again, and for some reason, Brielle didn't think he was joking.

Brielle tucked her purse under her arm, pushed Big D out of the way, and jumped into her car. It all happened so fast that Big D didn't realize what had happened. He just knew she was inside her car with the gear shift in reverse. Brielle began to back up the car, and Big D hurried out of the way. Brielle was so upset that there was a huge possibility that she would run over him, and he wasn't taking any chances.

Brielle made her way out of the parking garage. She was trying to get her thoughts together, but the smell of Big D's breath constantly reminded her of the dried saliva he had left on her face. She almost vomited again.

Instead, she heaved, rolling down the car windows, trying to catch her breath. Her temples were aching, and her throat was on fire. She searched her purse for a mint, gum—anything that could get the horrible taste out of her mouth. Her stomach convulsed, and it didn't help that she hadn't eaten anything all day. She found an old peppermint in the bottom of her purse. She quickly opened it, tossing it in her mouth.

Her purse vibrated. She looked at the screen. It was a message from Niko. She swiped the screen, but the tears in her eyes blurred her vision. Finally, she wiped her eyes and inhaled. A wave of nausea overcame her. She began praying not only for forgiveness but also hoping Big D hadn't given her some nasty mouth disease from his grimy mouth.

# Chapter 18

The following day, Damond sat in his office, studying the Public Utility Commission report from the last quarter. Quentin had explained to him how the rate changes would affect the call volume and how they may need to staff up before the rates hit the bills. Damond tried his best to listen to him, but his mind kept running back to his breakfast date with Niko. Going back for seconds was something that he had rarely done before. However, he had already made plans for Niko to have more of him. He usually never wanted a second encounter with a woman. They would typically get caught up in their feelings and blow up his phone, but Niko had not returned his texts or calls.

Quentin's cell phone rang. He nodded to Damond and walked out the door, taking the call.

Q never mentioned his intimate night with Niko to anyone and was hoping the call was her asking to link up again sometime soon. He looked at the caller ID and saw it was his brother calling. She hadn't called or texted him either. He answered with disappointment.

"Hey, man, what's up?" His brother wanted them to hang out later. Q needed this guy time because he wanted to vent about Niko. "Yeah, I get off at five, and I will meet you there . . . Nah, I'm good. OK, cool . . . Later!"

Damond had promoted Quentin to project manager, and just like anything Quentin was given, the dude was excelling at that. Yeah, Q was his boy, but he was also qualified for the position and good for the company. He knew there were rumblings on the floor, but there was also support for Q as well. His performance as the top-tier leader was on point every year. He implemented processes that produced positive results and significant successes for Charlotte Power. He had also recently completed his Six Sigma Black Belt certification. On paper, Quentin danced around the others, and everyone knew it. The truth was that, unlike Sean, Quentin was smart and overqualified.

Damond knew he needed to keep Q with him and ensure his career path matched his determination and skill. He was all about his business, and usually, Damond was on point as well, but with the arrival of Treasure, he was becoming distracted. His personal life and business priorities were also being distracted.

Damond had managed to convince Tia to stay with her people another week. He promised her he would be there to see them the upcoming weekend. He had already conjured a lie that he would tell her when he called to tell her he wouldn't be able to come. He needed to be with Niko again; this time, he needed her to make him feel like he did the night of his bachelor party.

Damond leaned back in his large, black leather office chair and sighed. The need to see this girl again was worse than it was years ago. He needed to get it out of his system, and it had to happen this weekend.


Angie zipped her sky-blue slacks and checked herself in the mirror. She worked so hard at being confident. She was the girl that everyone laughed at and picked on in school. The plain girl that didn't date in high school, and the girl that guys would have sex with or only hang out at her place with. She was never privileged to be taken out and seen in public with them. Angie had always been socially awkward. Her parents were loving and support-ive. They always tried to make sure she had everything she wanted and needed. Academically, Angie excelled in receiving a full scholarship to Spelman, graduating elev-enth in her class with honors. However, she had never had a serious relationship with anyone. Angie was very attractive, but with her controlling, rude, and uptight persona, men were not attracted to her. So they never wanted to stay around for any length of time, especially not long enough to commit to a relationship with her.

She placed an extra outfit and workout gear in her blue gym bag, grabbed her handbag and keys, and rushed to work. When she arrived, she heard laughter from the cubicle beside hers. As much as Torry didn't like her, he was not going to look at her nasty, period-stained pants all day long. Besides, this was the perfect opportunity for him to embarrass her even more than he usually would.

"Ummm, Angie, you need to excuse yourself to the restroom," Torry said while looking down at her slacks, hinting that something was wrong.

Angie looked down and took off, running toward the ladies' room. Tiffany took off behind her to check on her. Angie was embarrassed that Tiffany found her crying. Instead of appreciating Tiffany for being the only one to check on her, Angie snapped at her, then left the restroom. She took the stairs down to the lower level and ran to her car.

Angie checked her watch, noticing she had been gone from the floor for forty minutes. "Get it together," she muttered to herself.

She took a step, and a shooting pain shot through her ankle and foot. "Oh, ow." She lifted her leg and saw that her ankle was swollen. She was so angry and embar-rassed that she hadn't realized she twisted her ankle and didn't feel the pain. She couldn't believe she had hurt herself again at work.

"Angie? You okay?" Emery Adams, the HR assistant, asked as she got out of her car and walked toward Angie. "That ankle doesn't look good. Come on, we need to fill out some paperwork and get you to a doctor."

"No, no, I don't need a doctor. I just need some ice and elevation. I can do all that at my desk," Angie said as she attempted to take another step but stumbled. She had already been down this exact road before and didn't feel like going through the whole process again.

Big D sat at the front desk, licking the cheese off his fingers from the chili cheese fries he had shoved into his mouth. Helen, his coworker, watched in disgust as he smacked his lips and belched out a foul odor of onions and whatever other monstrosity he had devoured.

"You know, you should try to add some vegetables to your diet, Darryl. You can't keep eating like that and expect to live a long, healthy life," Helen said as she sprayed a floral scent into the air, trying to get rid of the stench emanating from Big D.

"Listen, my daddy eat just like me, and so did my granddaddy. They still eating fatback and grits every morning for breakfast, and they still kicking, licking, and sticking. Shoot, I bet my great-granddaddy ate like that too, but he dead, though." Big D reared back in the chair, laughing as loudly and obnoxiously as possible. "Big D come from good stock," he said, rubbing his stomach, letting out a foul-smelling belch. "Ha-ha. Anyway, thangs 'bout to change for me pretty soon. You gonna see a new Big D real soon. Yeaaaah, I got me a pretty li'l young thang looove every ounce of Big D. Umm-hmm."

Helen was usually good at blocking out just how gross Big D was, but how he hung on his words describing his newfound love and the thought of all his funk up against another person made her sick to her stomach. "*You* got a girlfriend?" Helen couldn't believe what she was hearing. She needed to see the person willing to give D and all of his funk a chance.

"Well, that what she want it to be, but you know they gots to earn me," Big D said, picking the cheese from the fries out of his teeth and eating it.

Helen turned away. She didn't want to laugh in his face, and she also didn't want to see Big D eating the remnants from the chili cheese fries lodged in his brown teeth. She imagined any woman wanting to be with Big D must be on the highest potency of crack cocaine or crystal meth.

Big D pulled out his phone and began talking to the picture while watching the video. "There go my baby right there with her fine ass. *Dayum,* I'm winning."

"Wow . . . Wait. So you got a picture of her, Darryl?" Helen asked, trying to keep a straight face.

"It's just for me . . . It's just for me," D answered, quickly closing the phone before Helen could sneak a peek. "You don't need to be all up in my business like that anyway. Don't worry, though. Big D still got enough to go around. You want soooome?" he teased Helen.

Helen shook her head vigorously while she continued writing the reports for the first half of the day. Big D groaned as he heaved his large butt up off of the stool. Then he stretched and walked around the counter. He needed to go pee again.


Brielle logged off her system for the day. She had managed to get through the day without encountering Big D, but not the thought of his repulsive tongue in her mouth. For some reason, aiding people in resolving their issues helped her not to concentrate on her current situation.

While packing up her things, she made eye contact with Niko. She didn't want to ignore Niko completely, so she smirked as if to say *later*. She desperately wanted to share with Niko what Big D had done, but she knew Niko would flip, ultimately exposing their sexual encounters as well as what Big D had done. Niko smiled back at her.

Brielle took out her phone and texted Mark that she would be working overtime and then going to the library, which was a lie. She checked her text messages, worried there would be some threats from Big D since she hadn't shown up the night before. Luckily, there was nothing from him. She walked nervously over to Niko's cubicle. She decided she couldn't hold it in any longer and felt that Niko would have a better sense of how to handle everything, so she determined to just come out with it.

"You got a moment? I need to talk to you about something," Brielle said with her voice trembling.

Niko could tell something was wrong. She knew that Mark was probably still giving her a hard time about her obligations as a wife since the CIAA incident. But something in Brielle's eyes told Niko it was more than just Mark.

Niko wasn't finished with her calls for the day, but she locked her system and motioned to Torry that she was taking a break. She grabbed her cell phone and walked silently down the hall with Brielle.

"Hey, boo, what's wrong?" Niko asked, pushing Brielle's hair behind her ear. "If you don't want to go home, come to my place. You know you're always welcome. Go get the baby and hang out with me for a little while." Niko wasn't focused on having sex with Brielle, although she couldn't stop thinking about how good it was. This time, she was more concerned with just sharing some time with Brielle to try to understand why she had been so distant.

The elevator dinged, and the doors opened. Brielle hoped Big D wasn't sitting in the lobby or near the parking garage.

"Brielle?" Niko was trying to snap her out of the daze that she was in.

The elevator door opened to the second floor, leading to the parking deck. Niko was about to step off the elevator, but Brielle pulled her back, hitting the button to the first floor and letting the door close.

"I didn't park here. I parked outside today." Brielle spoke as she tried not to look into Niko's eyes. She could feel herself tearing up.

The elevator door opened to the first floor, and, fortunately, Big D was nowhere in sight. Brielle scurried past the front desk toward the front door without looking at the security station. Niko was trying to keep up with her.

Outside, Brielle let her first tear drop from her eyes. Niko's heart started racing because she was clueless about what was happening. She could see Brielle's car parked five cars away, which was odd for Brielle to park on the street, especially during the week. Brielle was shaking as the tears were streaming down her face.

"Bri, what's wrong? Tell me." Niko was getting flustered because she hated seeing Bri upset. "Let's go sit in your car and talk."

Brielle unlocked the doors and looked around before getting into the car. Niko sat in the passenger's seat, taking Brielle's hand in hers.

"Please talk to me, Bri. I care about you more than you know. If it's Mark, you can leave him and stay with me. You don't have to put up with his controlling ways." Niko pleaded with her to share what was wrong. She didn't want to be the reason for Brielle and Mark's breakup, but she also wouldn't mind coming home to Brielle every day.

"You know, it's nothing . . . I'm just overreacting and tired. Let me drive you to your car." Brielle drove up the street into the parking garage when her phone buzzed. She stopped at Niko's white Nissan and smiled.

Niko looked around to see if anyone was near. Then she kissed Brielle while looking into her eyes. "You know you can talk to me, right?" Brielle nodded her head. "Text me when you get home, okay?" Brielle nodded a second time.

She waited for Niko to enter her car and then drove down the aisle. She pulled into one of the spaces and checked her cell phone.

Come to the back of the parking garage. I want me a little taste fo' you go home.

It was a text from Big D. Apparently, he had been watching her leave, and she didn't know it. Brielle felt her mouth begin to water, and she could feel her stomach churning. She broke out in a cold sweat. She placed the phone on the car seat and rested her head on the steering wheel. Reluctantly, she placed the gear into reverse, backed out of the space, and drove toward the back of the parking garage.

She drove to level six, which was empty. She saw Big D's massive ass standing toward the wall of the garage. She gripped the steering wheel and contemplated running him down with her car. Instead, she parked near him, and he pulled on the door. Brielle shook her head. There was no way his funky ass was getting in her car. She had cloth seats, and she could imagine the odor he would leave lingering in her car.

She opened the driver's door and stepped out. "You are not getting in my car . . . And what do you want? I haven't had the chance to get the money for you yet. I'll have it for you tomorrow," Brielle said, clutching her mace in her purse.

"I know you gonna get daddy his money. I ain't even worried about that, but I do want you to show me something. I needs to feel them big-ass titties in my mouth," Big D said, grinning at her with his coffee-stained teeth and black gums, still with particles of chili cheese fries caked on his teeth.

"*What?*" Brielle bellowed as she stepped back toward the car. "You have lost your mind."

"Look, what you gonna do is . . . You gonna git rid of that stank-ass attitude you got, and you gonna do what daddy like. You and that other bitch. Matter fact, did you tell her what I said? I'ma make sho y'all asses know who yo' king is. Now, I said I wanna taste them long nipples, and you best get to doin' what I ask, or some news stations, churches, and yo' husband gonna get some entertainment."

Brielle swallowed. She looked around to see if anyone was nearby. She wondered if it would be easier just to confess to what she had done and ask for forgiveness from Mark, or to go through with Big D's demands. She sighed and began to unbutton her blouse. She had on a white lace bra, and her DD breasts spilled out the top of it.

Big D rubbed his hands together. His heavy breathing sounded more like a dog than a man breathing hard. "Whoo, I ain't neva seen no titties like this be'fo. Damn, girl, them thangs is much prettier and juicier up close."

"Can't you just take the money? Why are you doing this, D?" Brielle said, closing her blouse.

"'Cause I can, bitch . . . And didn't nobody tell you to close that shit. Sit up on the hood of this car." Big D couldn't take his eyes off Brielle. It was almost like he had X-ray vision.

Tears began to roll down Brielle's face, and her stomach gurgled. Big D waddled over to her. His rancid breath raped her nostrils and slammed against her face.

"Ooh, yeah. I bet these jokers taste so fucking good." He grabbed Brielle's waist and covered her left breast with his nasty mouth.

Brielle tried to pull away, but he bit down on her nipple. He sucked her nipple in his mouth and pinched her right one.

Brielle began to sob as Big D's rough tongue and teeth assaulted her nipple. He was mumbling something. Having his mouth on her body made the lining of her stomach burn. She closed her eyes and thought back to the night that she and Niko made love.

Then Big D made a guttural sound and squeezed her ass. She kicked him back and ran to the side of her car to vomit. Her stomach convulsed twice, and she felt like she was going to die from vomiting. Brielle opened her back door and grabbed Misty's diaper bag. She spotted some Lysol disinfectant wipes beside the bag and grabbed those instead. Quickly, she scrubbed her nipples and breasts.

Big D was leaning on her car. "Damn, you done almost made me come in my pants, girl," he said, nearly out of breath.

"Get you funky, fat ass off my fucking car before you dent it!" Brielle yelled as she closed her blouse. "Move!" Brielle pushed her way back through to the driver's side.

"I ain't tell you that you could go."

Brielle opened the car door, but Big D slammed it closed. "I said you *almost* made me come. Now, make Big Daddy come. Put yo' hand in there and feel how blessed you is."

# Chapter 19

Niko sat on the couch of the hotel room. She sighed as she looked through her IG page and checked her text messages. She had hoped that Brielle would have called or texted her by now. She knew something was wrong with her, but she wouldn't tell her anything for some reason. She went to her Facebook page. Someone had tagged her in a video. She clicked on the notification icon and saw Angie's fall remixed to "No Flex Zone."

"This boy know he is crazy," Niko said as she watched the clip. She texted Torry, telling him that he was insane.

Chile, I was not the only one who recorded that shit, honey. I am on the floor laughing too at all these remixes, baby. What you doing anyway, bitch? You wanna go get some dranks? Torry replied.

He was so much fun to hang with, and she would take any opportunity to hang out with him. I'm handling some business at the moment. I'll get back at you in a li'l bit . . . Smooches, she texted back.

Niko stood and stretched. She was hungry as hell. She had let Damond talk her into meeting him at the hotel. She had sexed his ass into a coma. He had laid his phone on the table. She looked back into the room to make sure he was still asleep. Being with this dude had its benefits. She had used his phone to text Brielle again, hoping to keep Mark's suspicion minimal.

Brielle had asked whose number she was texting from. Niko told her it was a friend's phone and to make sure she responded to any text from that number unless Niko texted first.

Niko's phone buzzed. It was a message from Q.

I need to see you tomorrow. Stop by my place around noon.

Damond walked out of the bedroom. Niko sat fully dressed on the couch, looking at her phone. "I was just about to leave. I need to go meet some friends," Niko said as she stood.

"You . . ." Damond stopped himself from finishing the sentence. He didn't want Niko to leave, but he couldn't be a bitch-ass dude about it, either. She had delivered as promised, and he didn't want to be greedy, although he honestly wanted to.

Niko checked her hair in the mirror and applied cocoa-brown lip gloss to her soft lips. Damond felt his heart beating faster, and his palms began to sweat. He could not be falling in love with this girl. Shit, if he was, it was a foreign feeling to him. Love wasn't an emotion he understood or ever thought he felt.

His childhood, by most standards, was not traditional. His mother was more of a sister than a mother to him. They had even partied together when he was in college. He never had a curfew in middle or high school, and she allowed him to do as he pleased. The only rule in her house was that he had to maintain a high grade-point average, graduate high school, and attend college.

Damond's parents had divorced when he was 8. His father would stop by and visit after the divorce, but over time, he would visit less and less. Looking back on it, his mother had grown bored with his father and initiated the divorce. His father was heartbroken and still pursued her, until he realized he was fighting a losing battle for her heart.

Damond recalled hearing his mother say, "Your father is the ideal man for any woman. He is just not ideal for me." As he watched Niko walk out the door, he looked in the mirror and, for a brief moment, he recognized the look on his face was that of his father's when he left their house for the last time.

Damond, Quentin, Sean, and Nelson stood by the fountain at the Moss Museum. It was their monthly meeting of the 100 Black Men of Charlotte. Mark stood across the room sipping ginger ale and listening to Reverend Tillman congratulate him on his successful clothing line. Its launch was next week. Mark watched the men talking by the fountain and moved closer to them to hear their conversation.

"This dude right here must have the strongest back in America," Sean said, smacking Damond on the back. "He knocks 'em down, and he only gets top-shelf ass."

"Women ain't nothing but little girls looking for someone to tell them they're pretty and wanted. It's that's simple. Y'all niggas try too damn hard, trying to be witty and shit. That's y'all problem . . . KISS it, nigga. Keep It Short and Sweet." Damond laughed with the boys, sticking his chest out, proud of being known for smashing the most chicks as a married man.

Mark checked his phone. He had called the number he got from the text on Brielle's phone several times. He kept getting the voicemail and got Damond's name from the voicemail's personal recording. He googled him from his smartphone, only then realizing he was the SVP of CP&L customer care, the place where his wife was employed. Mark stared at the picture on his phone and looked at the guys standing across from him.

Damond was laughing and continued describing his exploits at work . . . in disturbing detail. Mark flexed his hand as he thought about how a predator like this had been pressuring Brielle to have an affair. Her lack of experience made her an easy target for this piece of shit.

Damond walked away from the group, and Mark followed him. Damond made several stops among different groups of men before heading into the restroom.

Mark paused before heading inside the bathroom behind him. *Should I be doing this? Will this make things worse by confronting this man?* he thought before inhaling and placing his hand on the knob . . . and turning it.

He stood in the bathroom stall, listening to Damond speak with someone on the phone. From the conversation, it sounded like he was speaking to his wife. Mark knew he was married from his research on him just that quickly through Google and Facebook. He stayed in the stall as he listened to Damond trying to convince his wife to extend her stay with her mother, again promising he would come down to spend time with them next week.

Damond's next call was to someone who didn't answer the phone. He heard him leaving a message stating that he wanted to see the person this weekend and make sure she was available. He had something special planned.

Mark wondered if he was calling Brielle. As he thought about this dude manipulating his wife, his head began to pound. He walked out of the stall and glared at Damond, who had a puzzled look on his face.

"You need something, man?" Damond asked as he washed his hands.

Mark took a deep breath. His hands were itching in a way that he had never felt before. "Yeah, I do, as a matter of fact. You know you are the worst type of dude. I mean, did your mother not teach you that you shouldn't play with other people's things? There is no point in me quoting the word of the Lord to you because it is so obvious that you don't know who He is by how you live your life."

Damond dried his hands and laughed. He had been confronted by more than one husband in his day, and it always played out with him being threatened. Occasionally, he had even ended up with a black eye, a split lip, and a broken nose.

"Look, if your wife and I have had some fun together, that's all it was. Trust me. I'm sure she learned a trick or two. You should be thanking me, bruh. It's now benefitted you in your bedroom," Damond said, winking. "Don't worry, I won't charge ya." He began to walk out the door when Mark grabbed his arm.

"Stay away from my wife," Mark threatened with piercing eyes.

Damond jerked his arm loose. "Look, I don't hit 'em more than once, so you don't have to worry 'bout me taking your wife. Hell, I got one of my own." He laughed as he walked out the door.

Mark walked outside, realizing that there was no reasoning with Damond. He knew it was time to go with plan B. The Bible had given him the punishment for Damond and Brielle's actions. Although he was sure Brielle would ask for forgiveness when the time came, it was evident that Damond wanted no part of mercy or even to admit that he was wrong.

He positioned himself in the garage, where he would be able to catch his victim off guard and have some privacy.

Niko sliced some fruit for an evening snack and placed it on the lavender plate. Her doorbell rang, and her eyebrow raised. *Who just showed up unannounced at my place?* She went to the door and looked through the peephole. It was Brielle. She instantly opened the door.

"Hey, B, what's up? What are you doing here? Come in, come in," Niko said while reaching to hug her. "I was just making a snack. You hungry?"

Brielle embraced Niko, holding on to her, wishing she could only live in that moment of feeling close to her. Niko kissed Brielle's neck. She couldn't believe she had shown up at the house and was in her arms. Brielle moaned as Niko's soft hands found their way to her stomach.

"Mmmmm, you taste so good, Bri. Don't make me wait this long again to have you, and how did you get your ass out of the house tonight?" Niko was taken back to the reality that Mark must have been busy for Brielle to stand in her apartment.

Brielle began babbling. "Niko, I've been missing you so much. Mark had something he had to take care of. He's been talking all strangely about how we need to talk after he gets this 'distraction' out of the way. I took the baby to my mom's house, and I'm hoping he doesn't come home tonight with a bunch of drama. But right now, I got something bigger we need to talk about," she said, holding Niko's chin in her hand.

Niko looked into Brielle's eyes. She could tell this was serious. Her stomach tightened. Brielle led her over to the couch, and they both sat down. She took Niko's hand and told her about everything Big D had been putting her through over the last few weeks. Niko had to sit back as she listened to Brielle describe Big D's threats and forced action on her.

Niko pulled Brielle close to her. "See, this is how fat, nasty niggas gotta do. He gotta blackmail some pussy because his nasty ass don't get none. I can't believe he fucking touched you. I will fucking kill him!" Niko was in a rage at the thought of all the things Big D had been doing to Brielle. She was even more upset that Brielle had kept it a secret all this time. There was no way Niko would have allowed this to continue had she known sooner.

"Niko, no, we gotta be smart about this. I don't know what or who he has shown that video to." Brielle's phone vibrated. She looked at the screen, and a wave of nausea came over her.

"What?" Brielle said, putting the phone on speaker.

"Da fuck you think you talking to? I done told you 'bout that stank-ass attitude of yours. You best get yo'self humbled when you speaking to Big Daddy D."

Niko was about to curse Big D's fat ass out, but Brielle motioned for her to be quiet.

"Tomorrow night gonna be a big night for you and your sidekick. I want y'all asses over here at six sharp, and make sure you bring the stuff I told you to bring. We 'bout to get real freaky up in this bitch. Oh, and stop by the Shell station and brang me a twenty-piece hot wing and some brews too." Big D began laughing, which became a raspy cough that sounded like he was about to choke to death on phlegm.

The doorbell rang in the background. "Hold on. Hey, who dat? Come in."

Brielle could hear men talking in the background.

"Damn, nigga, when you gonna clean up this nasty-ass house?"

"Fuck you, nigga. When *you* gonna get a job? I gots me a new maid service coming over here tomorrow to handle this shit."

The men laughed.

"Uh, hello . . . You still there?" Big D returned to the phone to check if Brielle had hung up.

Brielle huffed, "Yes."

"I done told you 'bout that attitude. But look, you got the address? It ain't hard to find. I know y'all excited too. Shit, I know I am." Then he hung up.

Brielle swiped *end* on the screen. She walked over to the table and poured herself some seltzer water.

"Bri, why didn't you tell me this shit sooner? You didn't have to carry this load by yourself, baby. Besides, I know how to deal with niggas like this." Niko walked over to Brielle, wrapping her arms around her waist.

"What do you mean, 'deal with people like this'? I think that the two of us can reason with him, Niko." Brielle was still thinking in Christian mode, not realizing for Big D to leave her alone permanently, she was going to have to adopt the ways of the devil temporarily.

"Reason with him? Isn't that what you been trying to do the last few weeks with his fat, funky ass? Damn, this is why I hate niggas. This kind of shit right here."

Niko sat down at the dining room table. Although Big D turning that video over to Mark would free Brielle, she didn't want to have Brielle's reputation destroyed, or Mark's either, for that matter. Even though Mark didn't deserve Brielle, he was still their child's father and a great provider for them. A scandal like this could drive a person over the edge.

"This musty-ass mammoth is playing with dynamite." Niko stared at her phone. She located her contacts list and searched for a name. Her finger hovered over Moose's phone number. One call to him and their issue would be resolved. Big D's funky blackmailing ass would be a distant memory.

# Chapter 20

The burning smell of the smoking gun flowed up into his nostrils along with the warm night air. He thought it was appropriate. It mirrored the rage that had consumed his mind for the last few hours—his marriage had deteriorated into a cold and godless union. Lying prostrate before him was the writhing body of the man who had stolen his life from him; robbed him of everything that he'd worked so hard for. He stood there emotionless, watching the thief tremble while begging him not to shoot again. His words sounded like the low moans of a wounded animal.

"Please! What are you doing? Please, don't kill me! . . . Please!" The man pled for his life as he struggled to breathe.

Looking down the smoked-filled barrel of the gun with the cold concrete of the parking garage closing in on him, he tried to reach out to Mark for mercy, but he was forced to put pressure on the wound. His blood was spurting onto the ground beneath him. Damond had always known that his arrogant lifestyle and womanizing ways would catch up to him someday—but he never imagined it to be like this. He felt the heat from the bullet as it seared through his stomach and out his back. He wondered if the guy standing over him just wanted him to suffer, or if he was really just such a lousy shot. The pain was like nothing he'd felt before.

Mark began to panic quietly and sweat profusely. His palms instantly became clammy. He'd come here to end this man's life for what he had done, and if he didn't finish him off, it would all be for nothing. The thoughts of his family, career, and life started flooding his mind. With his hand shaking, gripping the handle of the .22 Ruger, he stared at Damond for another second, then closed his eyes, took a deep breath, and pulled the trigger one last time.

Moose took a hit off of the blunt. He watched as the fat dude walked from the house to the car, opened the trunk to the old Cadillac DeVille, retrieved something, and then waddled back to his house. The large man wore a wife beater that would never again see its original color or size. Moose shook his head in disgust as he viewed the man's massive shape. He had a big, hard beer belly, man titties, and skinny-ass legs. Moose squinted as he tried to determine if the dude had socks on or if his feet were just that ashy. Moose couldn't stop thinking how this nigga was going to try to make his baby girl his damn sex slave. Nah, it wasn't even going down like that.

Niko had held him down so many times when others turned their backs on him. Hell, even her parents always had treated him like he was their son, more so than his own people. They had helped him finish school and open his auto shop. When he witnessed Niko drop a tear, that meant that a nigga would have to get dropped. She was a tough girl in his eyes, but he always told her that he would be the muscle for anything she needed. So when he got her text and then talked to her about what this dude was trying to do, he went straight into Mortal Combat mode.

He looked at the time, knowing his people would start showing up. The streetlight in front of the house blinked on and then off. Two figures walked across the street wearing all black. Moose laughed to himself and turned on his surveillance equipment. Just like Big D loved recording everyone else, his decoys were equipped with body cameras that would capture what was about to take place. Big D was finally about to star in his own debut and didn't even know it.

Moose could see the door of the fat man's house. He placed his earbud into his ear and opened the bag of salt and vinegar potato chips.

"Who is you?" Big D was looking through the peephole and asked the woman standing at his door.

"Niko and Brielle sent us," the lady's voice responded. "They said you wanted to party, so we here to party. Damn, I likes me a big boy. C'mon, open the door."

"Now, see, I told them girls to be here on time, not to send over nobody else," Big D said, still looking through the peephole.

"They on their way, but me and my girl here said we wanted to come and have fun too. This China, and I'm Monifah. You gonna make us stay outside till they come?" Monifah asked, pulling down the neckline of her shirt and exposing her voluptuous breasts. The flickering streetlight hit her nipple ring, and Big D's eyes almost bulged out of his head.

"Y'all, umm, damn . . . Y'all come in." Big D opened the door. "Damn, them some big-ass jugs you got. Shit. Y'all come on in here and quit teasing Big D," he said, holding the door for them.

The women laughed and walked inside. Big D grabbed the taller one's ass after she entered.

"You got a li'l fatty too. It's gonna be a party in this bitch with Daddy tonight, y'all," Big D said as he took one last look up and down the block before closing the door.

"Well, my daddy's name is Fred, and he lives in Florida," a male voice suddenly said as Big D turned around to meet the barrel of a gun in his face. "Damn, nigga, you got a body decomposing in this bitch? Get your big ass over there and sit down." The stench was of rotten potatoes and spoiled meat.

"Now, look. Y'all can take what you want. Just don't hurt me. Tell Brielle and Niko we cool, all right? Just don't kill me," Big D pled with the men.

"Shut the fuck up with yo' bitch ass. It's a li'l too late for all that shit now. And where the fuck is that li'l punk-ass phone of yours?" the man demanded.

Big D went to walk toward the table where his phone was lying when he felt a sting go across his back, which buckled his knees.

"Did we say move, you fat-ass pig?" Chi stood there holding a black whip.

"Did you just fucking hit me with a—" Big D could hardly get the words out before the whip came slashing down on him again. He let out a high-pitched scream.

The *"women"* laughed.

"Where is the phone, nigga?" Mo asked for the phone a second time.

"It's on the charger over there on the table." Big D was shaking, and his voice was trembling. He had no idea what was happening or what they planned to do to him.

Mo stepped over the black garbage bags and clothes. She grabbed the phone and went through the videos. She found the video of Niko and Brielle and then placed the phone in her back pocket.

"Bitch, I know you got this shit saved somewhere else." Mo walked over to the laptop that was sitting near the television. She plugged in the HDMI cables. The screen turned purple, then blue for a moment. Then the video popped up just where Big D left off watching it. Mo unplugged the laptop and set it by the door. "So, you like videos? Well, porky, you are about to be a star. Get yo' fat ass up. We need this apartment to be clean. It needs to be spotless for *our* video." Mo pointed toward the pile of clothes sitting on the floor.

Big D crawled over to the clothes and began to pick them up. He stared wide-eyed at the women, still confused about what was happening. He had kind of figured out that Niko and Brielle had something to do with it.

"Come on, Petunia, get your big ass up and get to cleaning. 'Cause after you clean, you got to make your debut. And if you act right, you can be the costar too!" Mo said, pulling up her skirt. Big D's eyes stretched so wide that they were about to pop out of his head.

Mark had not had a drink since he was elected to the deacons board many years ago. But this morning, he sat in the living room, sipping on some Hennessy, and it burned like hell going down . . . just like he was going to burn in hell for what he did last night. His memory was fuzzy after he left the restroom. He remembered standing behind the large SUV and the smell of gun smoke. The ride home had been a blur of lights and colors. He inhaled and swore he could still smell the gunpowder around him.

He took his drink and walked out to the patio. This was the second time in his life he had fired a gun to protect the woman he loved—once for his mother and now for his wife. Women were so naïve and needed to be protected, even if it was from themselves, he thought while closing his eyes, trying to convince his mind to delete the image of what he had done.

After Brielle had left that morning for work, he got up and took his truck to retrieve the gun. For once, he was grateful that his mother made him visit his great-uncle, Randy, over the summer. Randy felt all men needed to know how to handle a firearm properly. He taught him how to dismantle the pistol. He had found a skull cap, dark shades, and a jacket that he didn't remember owning in the front seat of his truck as well. He started the grill and placed the items he had worn in the flames. He nursed the fire until every bit of the evidence was gone.

Mark thought about the Bible and the readings about purgatory and how it was part of the damnation that his soul was now heading toward.

Brielle opened the door to Niko's car. She had made it to work an hour early because Niko said she had something important to show her. She had gotten Misty ready for daycare and placed Mark's breakfast in the microwave. It was unusual for him to be asleep when she left for work. He looked so peaceful that she decided not to wake him.

"Girl, I have something to show you," Niko said, smiling. She swiped the screen of her cell phone.

"My name is Darryl," Big D said while standing before a bed. He had on a black bra and fishnet pantyhose. Someone handed him a ruler. He placed his dick near the side of the ruler as the camera zoomed in. The head of his dick barely reached three inches.

Brielle could not believe her eyes as she watched Big D dance around to Beyoncé while spanking his own butt with a paddle and saying, "Owww, yeah. Y'all loving watching Big D's booty bounce." He even took and licked his nipple while wearing the bra. Brielle had to look away the last few minutes of the video as Big D serviced some faceless man with his crusty lips.

"Oh my God . . . Niko, how did you?" Brielle covered her mouth in disbelief as Niko laughed.

"Don't ask no questions, and I won't tell you no lies. But I bet his big, funky ass will *not* be bothering us again. Come on. Let's go inside and get some breakfast from the cafeteria," Niko said, kissing Brielle's hand.

The two walked in with their arms interlocked. On their way inside the building, they passed Angie on crutches. Brielle said good morning to her, but, of course, Angie didn't speak. The women giggled and headed toward the large glass doors of the building.

"Good morning, Helen," Niko said cheerfully. "How was your weekend?"

"It was good, Ms. Garcia. Looks like you ladies had a good weekend as well," Helen said before sipping her coffee.

"We did, we did," Niko replied, looking over at Big D. "And good morning to you too, Darryl. How was *your* weekend?"

Big D kept his head down, but the women could see his split lip and black eye. He mumbled something but continued pretending to be working on some reports.

"He had a terrible fall this weekend," Helen said. "I told him to go home and rest, but he won't listen."

The women noticed the familiar funk was not emanating from his direction. His shirt was a lighter shade of beige, and there was no usual morning crust in the corners of his eyes. He actually looked a few shades lighter than usual.

Brielle covered her mouth as she recalled the video of him being in the shower, washing, and how black the shower was after he got out. The video showed him wearing a pink shower cap and purple silk robe as he cleaned and scrubbed the shower after getting out.

"Feel better?" Niko said as she pulled Brielle toward the elevator. They stood silently, waiting for the doors to open. Once inside the elevator, the women could not contain their laughter. They both hollered out, laughing uncontrollably.

The elevator stopped at the second floor, and Quentin got on. The two toned down their laughter and noticed that Quentin was not in his usual, friendly mood.

"Good morning, Q. Are you all right?" Niko asked.

"Yeah, tough weekend?" Brielle asked, looking at him.

"You guys haven't heard?" Quentin said, holding the door as it opened to the sixth floor.

"Heard what?" Niko said while she adjusted the strap of her tote bag on her shoulder.

"About Damond. He was shot this weekend. They don't expect him to make it."

# Chapter 21

The call center floor was quiet, meaning there was little side chatter between calls. Niko stared at the monitor as the customer babbled on and on about her services being interrupted before she could pay her bill. Her mind was still reeling from the news she had just received from Q about Damond being shot. If this had happened in her former life as a stripper, she would have been a little shocked, but it would have been kind of expected, especially with her circle of friends at the time. But having something like this happen in the "normal" world was disturbing her to her core. This was a new life, a safe life, she thought, away from shit like people being shot.

Quentin had given them an update. He was told that Damond was barely hanging on. Niko immediately thought of his wife and kids, and then she thought about herself. She had dudes try really hard to please her before, but Damond's attempts were overkill. Still, she had to admit she loved the attention and the lengths he went through to reserve time for them. She looked over at Brielle, who was reading a book, and although Niko had strong feelings for Damond, it was nothing like what she felt for Brielle.

"Why the fuck did this happen to my nigga? Yo, this is some fucked-up shit!" Quentin fought back tears while talking to Sean. He paced the floor, upset that some coward would shoot Damond and leave him for dead. "They say that the camera didn't even get a clear picture of what happened. I bet if it were some white executive, these muthafuckas would be all over it."

"Calm down. I don't think race has anything to do with it, man. They are working with what they got," Sean told Q, trying to get him to keep cool. "Right now, we need to be there for Tia and the kids," Sean said, walking over and looking out the window.

Someone knocked on the door. Angela entered, and her eyes were swollen. She was wiping them with a tissue as she smiled weakly at Quentin. "I was just wondering if there had been an update on his condition?" she asked.

"No, Angela, there hasn't been any change. He's still in ICU fighting, and his surgery is still scheduled for today," Quentin said as he walked over and patted her shoulder.

Angie tried to fight back her tears. "Do the police know anything?"

"We haven't heard any further updates yet. Just tell everyone we'll let them know as soon as we know something, okay?" Sean was getting frustrated with Angie's questions.

Angela nodded and left the office.

Quentin shook his head and pulled out his cell phone. "I'm calling Detective Marshall now. I need to find out if they have any further information." He pulled the detective's card from his pocket.


Niko and Brielle hardly said anything to each other all day. Now, it was the end of the day, and everyone was packing up to leave.

"Hey, guys, I'm heading over to the hospital. Y'all want to ride along?" Quentin asked while staring at Niko. His best friend was in the hospital fighting for his life, but

Q saw this as the perfect opportunity to get some alone time with Niko.

"Yes, we would . . . We would love to come. I'm sure his wife can use all the support and prayer she can get," Brielle said before Niko could answer.

Quentin was hoping that Brielle would have to get home to her husband and would pass up the opportunity. Instead, she answered for both of them, taking Q up on his offer to take them to the hospital.

"Oh, okay. Well, come on," Quentin said, stepping back so the women could lead the way to the elevators.

Niko hated the smell and the feeling of hospitals. The fluorescent lights beamed down on them as they walked down the hallway to the waiting area. A woman wearing a white cotton T-shirt, jeans, and some white Nike Air Max sat in one of the green chairs. Her microbraids were pulled back in a messy ponytail. She was chewing on her bottom lip and was staring at something no one else could see.

"Hey, beautiful," Quentin said as he walked into the waiting room and sat beside the woman. She continued to stare off into space as Quentin took her hand. Brielle walked over and sat on the woman's other side in the empty chair.

"Mrs. Wilks, I am so sorry this has happened. If you would like, we can pray together. I know it seems dark, but God has a plan, and we must trust Him to bring Mr. Wilks through this." Brielle put her arm around her. Tia fell over on Brielle and began to sob.

"I don't know what to do if he doesn't make it. I don't understand why this happened to him." Tia sobbed uncontrollably as Q and Brielle tried to calm and console her. "I knew something bad was coming. I have been feeling it for the last two months. Something just didn't feel right. I prayed for protection and wisdom, hoping God would keep us safe. I . . . I . . ."

"Mrs. Wilks," a petite woman said, walking over to Tia.

Niko turned and was unable to hide her shock as she watched them rolling what was supposed to be Damond out of a room on a hospital bed with all kinds of tubes and monitors coming from his body. His face was so swollen that he looked like he was wearing a horrible Halloween mask.

"We're taking him up for surgery now," the nurse said, helping Tia as she tried to stand. Brielle and Quentin helped to support her. She walked over to Damond and kissed his forehead.

"Do we have time to pray over him and your staff?" Brielle asked.

"Honey, we make time for the Lord," a Black nurse said, taking Brielle's hand.

Brielle looked at Niko, who was standing back. All the color had drained from her face, and she seemed terrified. Quentin walked over, grabbed Niko's hand, and pulled her closer to Damond.

Everyone held hands as Brielle prayed for Damond, the staff, and strength for his family and friends.


Brielle opened the door and kicked her shoes off. Mark walked down the stairs. Brielle didn't say a word to him at first. She walked into the kitchen and opened the refrigerator.

"Where have you been? I called you several times. You had me worried sick." Mark looked sternly at Brielle, awaiting a response.